Fortescue Fox

Strathpeffer Spa

Its Climate and Waters - With Observations Historical, Medical and General,

Descriptive of the Vicinity

Fortescue Fox

Strathpeffer Spa
Its Climate and Waters - With Observations Historical, Medical and General, Descriptive of the Vicinity

ISBN/EAN: 9783337142650

Printed in Europe, USA, Canada, Australia, Japan

Cover: Foto ©Andreas Hilbeck / pixelio.de

More available books at **www.hansebooks.com**

STRATHPEFFER SPA

ITS

CLIMATE AND WATERS

From a Photo. by V. Valentine & Sons, Ltd. Maclure, Macdonald & Co., Glasgow.

STRATHPEFFER SPA

ITS

CLIMATE AND WATERS

*WITH OBSERVATIONS HISTORICAL, MEDICAL,
AND GENERAL, DESCRIPTIVE OF THE VICINITY*

BY

FORTESCUE FOX, M.D. (LOND.)

FELLOW OF THE MEDICAL SOCIETY OF LONDON

ILLUSTRATED

LONDON

H. K. LEWIS, 136, GOWER STREET, W.C.

1889

To the Right Honourable

THE EARL OF CROMARTIE,

THE OWNER OF STRATHPEFFER SPA,

THIS BOOK

IS RESPECTFULLY AND BY PERMISSION DEDICATED.

PREFACE.

THE present little volume I address not only to Medical Men and others who are interested in Strathpeffer, but also to the Visitors at the Spa. My hope would be that the first class may find in it a contribution to the better knowledge of an important Health Resort; and that visitors may be able to derive, not only some guidance in their use of the Waters, but also pleasure, from the perusal of its pages.

In the essay **Strathpeffer Spa in 1887** it was not possible for me to offer more than rough outlines of a group of various topics. The same subjects are here dealt with in greater detail, and longer experience has enabled me to correct in some particulars, and enlarge in others, the conclusions first put forward. The lapse of time has also given opportunity for a much more thorough study of the Climate.

It is generally true that what is of casual interest

to all is of vital consequence to some. The Weather has been to all classes always a staple subject of remark : and now Climate, from the medical point of view, has come to occupy the position of a well-recognized and important branch of treatment.

From this it follows that the climatic peculiarities of a Resort demand in these days most careful scrutiny. For climatic conditions may, and do, impede or aid the use of waters, and especially of baths ; they modify the effects of the treatment in every particular, and they are often so commanding as in themselves to render a place suitable or unsuitable for certain classes of cases.

As no accounts of the *Strathpeffer Climate* have hitherto appeared, I make no apology for giving the subject a prominent place in this work. An authority more competent than myself has dealt in Chapter II. with a series of meteorological readings now extending over nearly five years. The various elements are carefully analyzed, and are compared with the records of the Royal Observatory for the same period.

Exact observation has in this manner established, *inter alia*, what general impressions long ago suggested, that Strathpeffer possesses an uncommonly mild and sunny winter climate. Regarded as a Winter Resort it is mild and yet bracing.

We have thus another illustration of a fact sometimes overlooked that there are many climates in the United Kingdom, varying greatly among themselves in exposure, temperature, and atmospheric conditions, and therefore in the amount of *available* sunshine. Those who seek refuge, or those who send others to seek refuge, abroad from the damp airs and fogs of the south of England, might instead very well and wisely make trial of a winter in the sunny but sheltered Highland valley of the Peffery.

As bearing upon this subject I must be allowed to express the hope that fir-trees in the neighbourhood of the Spa will in future be spared. Those who are familiar with these questions are aware that *pine-clad slopes* materially enhance, in more ways than one, the healthful character of a Climate. In the case of Strathpeffer, only carriage access is needed to make them in addition a great source of attraction to visitors. An exquisite winding drive might easily be led around the base of Cnoc Moir ; and, overlooking the Spa, pass onwards through a " palisade of pine trees," to the neck of Knock Farril.

The Medicinal Properties of the *Waters*, both Sulphur and Chalybeate, are dealt with at some length, both theoretically, and more practically, by the narrative of cases illustrating their use. It must be remembered that individual peculiarities very seriously modify almost every rule that can be laid down, and that no two cases, any more than two faces, are alike in all respects.

As in the case of climate, so here, it is necessary to protest against the common tendency to exalt foreign waters above our own. Many an "Old Hand" at Spa-going, who has tried near and far, ends by acknowledging with the poet :—

> A man's best things lie nearest him,
>   Even round about his feet :
> It is the distant and the far
>   That we are fain to greet.

The following pages would only partially fulfil their purpose if, having shown, however imperfectly, what Strathpeffer *is*, they did not in addition furnish some indication of what it *is becoming* and *is to be*. Much has been accomplished ; much is 'in process ; and much remains to be done at the Spa. Under the present rapid rate of growth, it is clear that a second Establishment, for Sulphur and Thermal Treatment, will soon be necessary ; and advantage will then no doubt be taken of well-ascertained principles, and of the many modern improvements and accommodations, which it is not always an easy matter to graft upon an older structure.

The capacities and resources of Strathpeffer are more than ample : they are capable of almost indefinite extension. The impending addition of Peat Baths is but one of many proper developments, either present or prospective. One further practical point may be here noticed. For winter accommodation, a suitable house should be erected on the sunny heights above the railway at Auchterneed.

In matters such as these it is that public spirit or private enterprise, as the case may be, is shown : and it is in enterprise and spirit, rather than in climate and waters, that the Home Spas have hitherto been excelled by those of Germany and France. The old warning remains true :—

> . . . our doubts are traitors,
> And make us lose the good we oft might win
> By fearing to attempt.

But there are signs that a new order is at hand. To use once more the words of the essay to which reference has already been made : "The resources of Nature are at length on all hands beginning to be aided by the resources of civilization, in such a manner as to extend and perfect the provision for Health in Waters and Climate. For such a development of these natural modes of treatment the hour is now ripe. Few others stand on a basis at once so rational and unquestioned, and none possess in like degree the promise of the future."

My best acknowledgments are due, for kind assistance in preparing the latter portion of the book, to Dr. Alexander Fraser of Marlborough, Mr W. F. Gunn of Strathpeffer, and Dr. Hingston Fox of Finsbury Circus. The reader will find in this portion some account of the excursions and scenery in the neighbourhood of the Spa, with miscellaneous notes upon objects of antiquarian, historical, and scientific interest.

EAGLESTONE : *April* 1889.

CONTENTS.

CHAPTER III.

THE CHEMICAL PROPERTIES OF THE SULPHUR WATERS.

CHAPTER IV.

THE MEDICINAL PROPERTIES OF THE SULPHUR WATERS.

CHAPTER V.

BATHS AND MASSAGE.

CHAPTER VI.

THE NEW CHALYBEATE SPRING.

CHAPTER VII.

ILLUSTRATIVE CASES.

CHAPTER VIII.

SPA LIFE AND DIET—THE "SEASON." STRATHPEFFER AS A WINTER RESORT.

PART II.—GENERAL.

CHAPTER IX.

EXCURSIONS.

b

Illustrations.

STRATHPEFFER SPA,

ITS CLIMATE AND WATERS.

PART I.—MEDICAL.

CHAPTER I.

HISTORICAL SKETCH.

SITUATED in the Highlands of Scotland, nearly twenty miles north-westward by rail from Inverness, is a broad valley between four and five miles in length. At its eastern extremity it opens on the seacoast at Dingwall. It is sheltered on the north by the broad shoulders of Ben Wyvis (3,429 feet); the more rugged and broken mountains of Ross-shire enclose the western end; whilst to the south the vale is bounded by the narrow ridge named, from its bristly contour Druim Chat, " The Cat's Back."

This is Strathpeffer—the Strath of the Peffery—a green and fertile valley on the eastern verge of a wild and rocky hill country. A cluster of grey stone houses nestles at its upper end, and this is Strathpeffer Spa, the subject of the present pages.

From the hills above it the eye ranges over the Black Isle and Cromarty Firth to the eastward, and to the west over a mountainous country broken by water-courses and interspersed with lochs. Once the scene of perpetual feuds, this country is now for the most part devoted to the peaceable pursuit of sport. Grouse moors and deer forests stretch for miles over the silent hills ; and the angler has taken possession of every stream. In Strathpeffer, the vale below, the change is still more striking : for the very spot where sanguinary clan con-flicts have been fought again and again has become, in a milder age, a Place of Healing.

Although in most cases Mineral Springs have been resorted to from early times, at all events by the sick of the vicinity, there is no record of any considerable use of the Strathpeffer waters much before the begin-ning of the present century. Hints are forthcoming of an earlier local fame, but what appears to be the first published account of the "Castle Leod Water" was communicated to the Royal Society in London in 1772, by Dr. Donald Munro, F.R.S.[*] "Having heard many gentlemen from the county of Ross speak of these waters," Dr. Munro asked for an account of them from "some physical person" in the neighbourhood. Dr.

---

[*] *Philosophical Trans.*, vol. lxii., p. 15.

Alexander Mackenzie of Tarbet forwarded him a description, in which he remarks :—" The bottom of the
well and of the channel . . . is black, as if dyed with ink ;
and the leaves of the alder bushes that fall into the well
soon contract a blackish colour ; . . . but when taken
out and dried appear covered with a whitish dust, which
is undoubtedly sulphur. . . . All that I can learn of the
operation of this water from some sensible people of
credit and observation, who have drunk it this as well as
former seasons, is, that it very sensibly increases the
action of the kidneys, and sometimes remarkably opens
the pores ; but I do not find from the report of any that
it purges, though drunk to the quantity of three, sometimes of four, English quarts in the day. Almost every
person remarks that it whets the appetite, and sits
light on the stomach. . . . Every person in the country
prescribes the water for themselves, and runs to the
well or sends for the water for every complaint, acute
and chronic. . . . Some very foul faces have been
quite cleared ; and at this time a gentleman's son, nine
years of age, with a herpes round the neck which had
proved extremely obstinate to other means, has got a
perfect cure by drinking and washing with them. . . .
Some foul ulcers on the legs, and one with every
appearance of a carious thighbone, have been perfectly
cured." Thus far Dr. Mackenzie.

By others Dr. Munro was informed that the waters
had "been used with success in many of those cutaneous
disorders commonly called scorbutic, and in curing the

itch." Dr. Munro describes experiments made upon
some samples of the water that had been sent to
him. . . . "A shilling and a sixpence put into two
different teacups were presently tarnished, and became
of a very dark colour. A watery tincture of galls
brought a variegated scum of the colour of a pigeon's
breast to the surface." The water was evaporated in
large stone basins, and the sediments, which were small,
very carefully tested. He found a soluble black earth,
an insoluble earth possibly selenite, a crystalline salt
apparently identical with Glauber salt, and a "small
pittance" of a yellow oily matter containing a perceptible proportion of sulphur.

He adds : " It appears that this is one of the strongest
sulphureous waters hitherto found in Great Britain. . . .
In its natural state it is impregnated with a volatile
sulphureous vapour, which evaporates soon when exposed to the open air, and flies off immediately when
exposed to heat. The water then loses its strong
sulphureous smell and taste. Also it lets drop to the
bottom of the well, and of its channels, a fine powder of
sulphur, which adheres to the leaves and branches of
trees found there. As this water contains but very
little purging salt and does not operate by the bowels,
sea-water, or some purging salt, may be added to the
first glasses drunk in a morning when purging is
required. Equal parts of the Castle Leod and sea water
mixed together make a water in most respects similar
to the Harrogate : and probably will be found to

answer in most cases where the Harrogate water has been found useful."

Five years after this was written, under the increasing demand made upon the Waters, some sort of accommodation for visitors became absolutely necessary. At that time the Estates of Cromartie, including Strathpeffer, were, with many others affected by the late Rebellion, still in the hands of the Crown. The Factor of Cromartie was then (1777) a Mr. Colin Mackenzie, a man who holds the honourable place of Pioneer in the history of the Spa. Recognizing the necessities of the case, Mr. Mackenzie drew up the following Memorandum, and forwarded it to the Commissioners of the Forfeited Estates :—

" The Memorial and Representation of Colin Mackenzie, Factor upon the Annexed Estate of Cromarty, humbly sheweth :

" That some years ago a fine Mineral Well was discovered on the lands of Ardival, in the Barony of Strathpeffer, a part of the said Annexed Estate of Cromarty ; and some of the country-people having, partly from curiosity and partly on account of some disorders they laboured under, continued to drink this water, it totally removed the complaints of such as were ailing. This circumstance drew the attention of several of the better sort of people to this Well; and Dr. Alexander Mackenzie, at New Tarbet, having made some experiments upon the water, sent some of it to Dr.

Donald Munro, at London, who, after making the proper
trial, wrote a short treatise upon its qualities, which he
gave into, and which stands recorded among, the
Transactions of the Royal Society, and in which treatise
it is said that by adding a little salts to this water, it is
at least equal, if not superior, to that of Harrogate.

" From almost daily and repeated instances, it is
certain beyond doubt that this water creates an appetite
and digestion, and is a remarkable cure for scorbutic or
other disorders in the blood, swellings, ulcers, etc. And
the memorialist knows of two instances—one of William
Smith, Master of the Grammar School of Fortrose ; and
the other of Angus Sutherland, tacksman, of Kincardine
—who were both so lame and feeble that they were
obliged to be carried to the Well on feather beds in carts ;
but by the use of the water for some weeks they so
far recovered as to be able to walk upon their own legs
for miles. From these and (the following) other favourable circumstances, the Strathpeffer Well has for these
five years past been pretty much frequented by different
ranks of people from the counties of Ross, Cromarty,
Inverness, Moray and Sutherland ; and last season there
were some from the town of Aberdeen.

" But the want of accommodation near the Well for
the better sort of people discourages many from coming
there that otherwise would attend. The memorialist
therefore, humbly submits to the Honourable Board
whether it would not be proper, for the encouragement
of ladies and gentlemen resorting to this Well, to build a

good House, Kitchen, and Stable—either upon the Farm of Kinettas, or upon the Lands of Ardguie, both of them dry, wholesome, well-aired places, commanding a fine prospect, and lying within a gunshot of the Well, abounding with agreeable and romantic walks, and having very fine goat pasture within half a quarter of a mile of them.

"This house would not only be a great accommodation to those frequenting the Well, but would be of great use to the tenants of the whole Barony of Strathpeffer. It would be the means of affording them a ready and good market during the summer and harvest seasons for what wares they have to dispose of; such as butter, cheese, eggs, milk, kid, lamb, mutton, and poultry; and would in general create such a circulation as to enable them to pay their rents more punctually than usual, and also to rear more of the above articles than they formerly did. Nor is it improbable that in time this place might become a thriving village.

"The minister of the parish caused to be erected a kind of building about this Well to preserve it from being abused by cattle, etc., which by no means answers the end proposed. But by laying out an expense of £5 or £6, a proper building might be erected that would preserve the Well from any abuse either from man or beast.

"It is of infinite service to numbers in this part of the world; and I wish to God half-a-dozen of the Honourable Board (for pleasure only) tried it for three weeks—

they would get an appetite, a pack of good hounds, and plenty of game, goat whey, etc. *Then* there would be little occasion for soliciting a support to the enclosed Memorial Representation. However, lame as it is, and far short of what might have been said by a proper hand for writing upon that subject, I beg to have the opinion of the Board upon it."

In consequence of these energetic representations, the Commissioners directed further investigations to be made and a report prepared. It was then discovered from geological examination, that water-bearing strata occurred in different parts of the valley, and that there were, not one but several powerful springs of Chalybeate and Sulphur water.

Having in this manner been brought into notice as a Spa, Strathpeffer attracted the attention of medical men and others in England and Scotland. But travelling was then slow and difficult. Old men still alive remember the month's journey from London with the Lairds' coach. Comparatively few therefore ventured into Scotland for mineral waters, and Strathpeffer naturally became the Spa of the northern counties, from the West coast, Lewis, and the far north to Aberdeen-shire in the east. "Great numbers," says a local writer in 1791, "from the counties of Inverness and Sutherland and the western districts of Ross-shire, have resorted hither."

Twenty years later, while the sulphur waters flowed

as before, the stream of popular favour appears to have suffered a temporary check, and Sir George Mackenzie, the philosophic proprietor of Coul, writes (1810) : " The once-famed virtues of the Strathpeffer Spring *are begin-ning to be neglected*. It has been celebrated for curing all sorts of diseases, particularly scrofula and diseases of the skin."

To the late Dr. Morrison, of Dunsaig in Aberdeenshire, belongs the great credit of again bringing Strathpeffer into the light of day, and establishing it in its rightful position as one of the acknowledged Health Resorts of the country. Acting on the old precept, *Physician heal thyself*, Dr. Morrison first found in his own case, after trying many remedies for a serious disorder, a complete cure from the use of these sulphur waters. Encouraged by this, and by many other examples of successful treatment, he lost no time in making the virtues of Strathpeffer known. He came to live near the Spa (Elsick Cottage), and exerted himself to raise a small Pump Room over the " Strong Well " in 1819, on the site of the present building. In the latter his portrait may still be seen and there are residents yet living who remember the antique dress and dignified bearing of the old Doctor.

Even after Dr. Morrison's time, however, the Spa long remained very deficient in necessary accommoda-tion. A recent visitor thus in his old age graphically describes his own experience between 1830 and 1840 : " I had heard of Strathpeffer, and I wanted to see what sort of a place it was. Riding out from Dingwall, I do not think I could find a feed for my horse or for myself, and I had to ride back again without."

All this was soon to be changed. The Mineral Wells, to which Baths were now added, were taken under the direct management of the Estate. In 1861 a strong stone Pump Room took the place of the old wooden building: a second story with new bath-rooms was added in 1871, and ten years later the range now known as the " Ladies' Baths " was erected. In the meanwhile, the successive extensions of the railway northward, to Inverness, to Dingwall, and finally by the branch line opened in 1885, to Strathpeffer itself, made it more accessible to the English invalid. Not only so, but they placed it in touch with the South : and so have brought, and are still bringing about that more perfect development of the resources of the Spa, which alone—and rightly so—can enable it to satisfy modern and scientific requirements.

The above furnishes but a faint outline of the one hundred and ten years' history of Strathpeffer ; but it exhibits the familiar features of slow beginning, varying fortunes, and under more favourable circumstances rapid growth. Moreover, in the case of Strathpeffer the progressive movement of the last decade perhaps exceeds the accumulated advance of the century. The earlier Workers and their work cannot be forgotten. They are worthy of all honour as leaders and examples. But one more recent name is entitled to rank with theirs, that of the late Dr. David Manson. He was the first (in 1866) to publish a systematic treatise on the Spa, and to his genius and enthusiasm are directly and indirectly due, not only much of the modern growth of Strathpeffer, but the benefit which thousands have derived from its waters.

Among the latest works of improvement may be named : A new system of Heating the Baths ; several large Reservoirs for the storage of sulphur water ; Douche Rooms fitted with various apparatus ; the introduction of Massage ; and, also, by a recent decision, of the Peat Bath. Like efforts are still in active continuance, under the enlightened supervision of Mr. Gunn, the Factor on the Estate, to whom the place is indebted for valuable services during many years.

The impulse of Development which in recent years spread like a wave over the Health Resorts of this country, was nowhere more powerfully felt than at Strathpeffer. The repeated presence of Cholera on the Continent, and, at the same time, the increased willingness on other grounds, of the medical profession and public to acknowledge the forgotten merits of the Home Spas, were no doubt the great causes of this movement. They afforded at the same time the best justification of an earnest endeavour, not only to extend and perfect, in all the methods approved by science, the precise administration of our Baths and Waters, but also to provide in a manner unknown before, increased and varied extraneous attractions.

That endeavour is not unworthy of support : for in these days, when the love of Nationality seems to be undiminished, the Spas of England, Scotland, Ireland and Wales, if they can show themselves favoured of Nature and not neglected by man, should surely not appeal to deaf ears.

Whether the northern Spa can make good any such claim, let the reader judge.

CHAPTER II.

THE CLIMATE OF STRATHPEFFER SPA.

[*Contributed by* H. COURTENAY FOX, M.R.C.S. ENG.,
late Fellow of the Meteorological Society of London].

IN the following pages it is proposed to summarize the principal features in the Meteorology of Strathpeffer, and to compare them with those of London and some other neighbourhoods. The observations on which the essay is based, have been regularly conducted by Dr. F. Fox from 1st November 1884. The instruments used are a Symon's five-inch rain gauge, well exposed, and Negretti and Zambra's standard maximum and minimum registering thermometers, which are placed in a louvred screen, well ventilated, on the north side of the house. The altitude is about 220 feet above sea-level.

The latitude of Strathpeffer Spa is 57°34′ N., or about six degrees higher than that of London. We should expect on this account to find the temperature generally cooler, the reduction being probably least in summer and greatest in winter, when the sun is near the horizon. By the kindness of a meteorological friend, who has

made the calculation for me, I am enabled to present the
following table giving the comparative values of solar
radiation at Strathpeffer and Greenwich.   The light and
heat received from the sun, moment by moment, during
the day (*excluding the effects of atmospheric absorption*)
are here expressed in terms of the number of seconds
that he would require to shine *in the zenith*, in order to
give an equal amount of radiation.

| | Length of Day, in seconds. | Zenith Solar-seconds. | |
		In seconds.	Hours and minutes (approximate).
SUMMER SOLSTICE—			
Strathpeffer . .	63,805	31,345	8 hrs. 42 min.
Greenwich . .	59,067	31,563	8 ,, 46 ,,
EQUINOX—			
Strathpeffer . .	43,200	14,777	4 hrs. 6 min.
Greenwich . .	43,200	17,120	4 ,, 45 ,,
WINTER SOLSTICE—			
Strathpeffer . .	22,595	2,341	0 hr. 39 min.
Greenwich .	27,333	4.649	1 ,, 17 ,,

It follows from this table that in summer the greater
length of the day in the more northern station nearly
compensates the loss of solar radiation involved in the
lower altitude of the sun.   That is apart altogether from
atmospheric conditions, which, in winter particularly,
mainly determine the available radiation.

Contrary to natural expectations, the Strathpeffer summer is much cooler than in the south of Britain, while, strange as it seems, the average winter temperature is very little lower than that of the neighbourhood of London, and some of the winter months have even been slightly warmer.

This result will not appear so surprising if we call to mind the principal conditions which determine the climate of the north of Scotland. First, *the proximity of the sea* is well known to temper the extremes of heat and cold, tending to produce cool summers and warm winters, and a more equable climate. Moreover, the sea—especially on the *western* coast of Scotland—is maintained at a relatively high temperature by the constant flow of the warm equatorial currents. "During the winter months," said the late Dr. Carpenter,—himself a visitor to Strathpeffer,—"there is a constant excess of sea-temperature above that of the air, averaging 6·2° Fahr., along the west coast of Scotland and its islands." The value of such a warm current in high latitudes is strikingly shown in the absence of ice in the harbours of Norway, even as far north as Hammerfest, through the whole winter.

Secondly, the *direction of the prevailing winds* is one of the most important elements of climate. Modern research has shown the frequent dependence of the weather upon extensive areas of low pressure, that successively approach from the Atlantic and pass over our islands in an easterly or north-easterly direction.

The winds are found to blow around and in toward the centre of these depressions, and the direction of rotation is against the hands of a watch. The character of the weather at any moment depends upon our position with regard to the central area of lowest pressure. If we are on the south side, the weather in winter is generally warm and wet, with south-westerly winds. But when the centre itself lies to the southward of us, we have cold and bleak north-easterly winds. The majority of these disturbances skirt our northern coasts, and hence we have in winter a preponderance of south-westerly winds, with warm rains on the western slopes of the mountains, while the south of England is not unfrequently linked on to an area of high pressure (anticyclone) which brings cold, dull, foggy and frosty weather.

Thirdly, the *aqueous vapour* present in the atmosphere keeps the earth warm like a blanket at night, and prevents those sudden changes of temperature that are so hurtful to animal and vegetable life.

Fourthly, between Strathpeffer and the western coast rises a *mountainous table-land,* which not only breaks the force of the Atlantic gales, but robs them of a large proportion of their moisture. I cannot do better than quote from an observant writer residing near the Spa in 1772 :—"It is worth remarking that the western mountains make the weather alternately foul and fair on the east and west borders of them, in some measure similar to the monsoons on the Malabar and Coromandel coasts.

Meteorology of Strathpeffer Spa, compared with Royal Observatory (Greenwich).

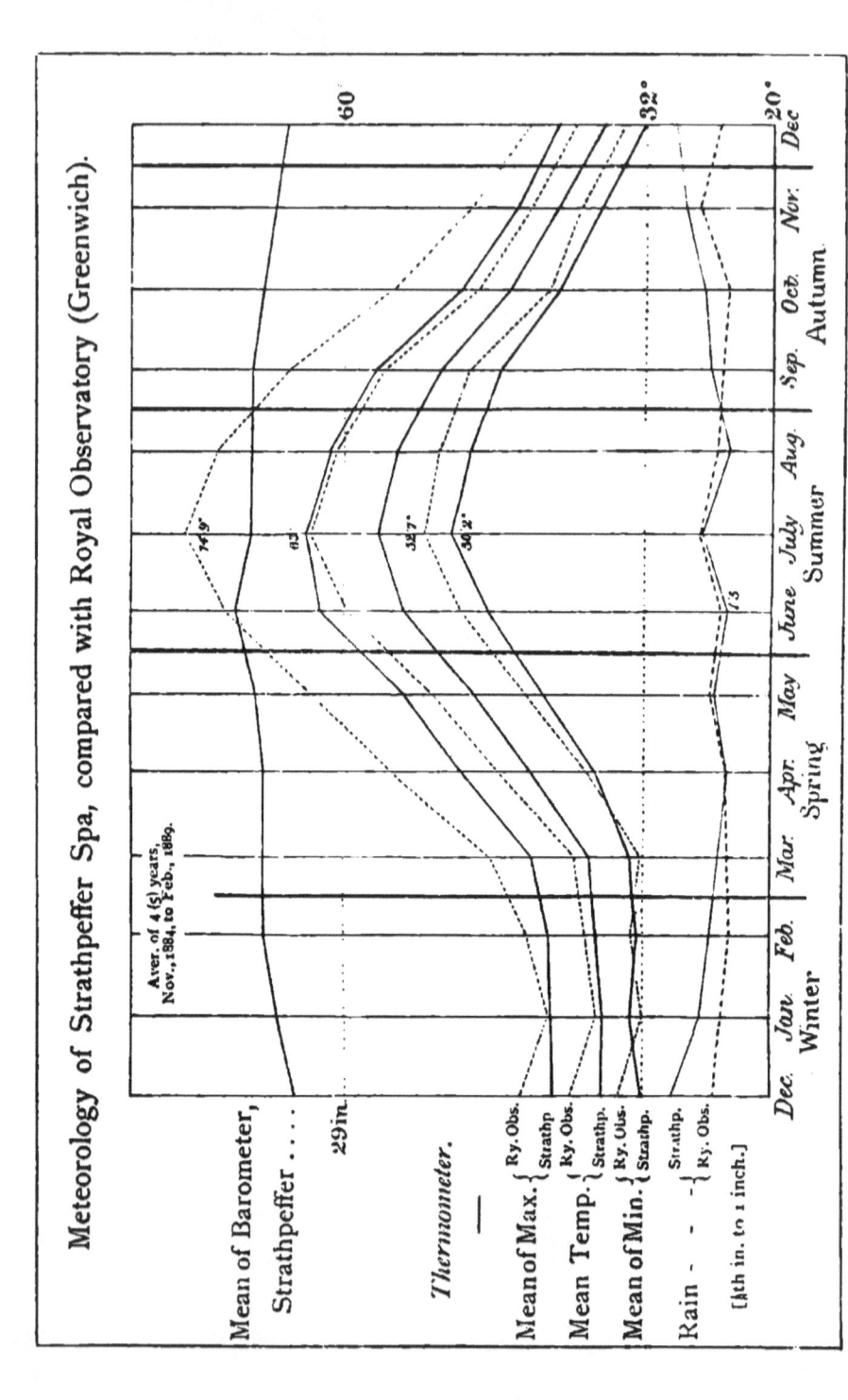

The west and south-west winds blow most frequently,
during which it generally rains on the west coast and is
fair weather on this side of the hills, or at most there
are only slight occasional showers. On the other hand,
the east wind uniformly [?] brings rain or sleet on the east
coast, but the storm dies away in the intermediate hills,
and there is dry weather and sunshine on the west coast." *

The accompanying **Diagram** exhibits at a glance the
mean value of some of the principal meteorological
elements for each month, on the average of four to five
years. The months are grouped into the usual meteorological seasons, and in order to give a complete view of
the winter, an additional column is given to December.
At the foot of the diagram the rainfall of Strathpeffer is
compared with that of the Royal Observatory, which, it
will be remembered is situated in one of the driest districts in England. Occupying the middle portion of the
diagram are three full curved lines, and three dotted ones,
showing, for Strathpeffer and Greenwich respectively, the
average of the low night temperatures and of the high
day temperatures, and also the mean temperature of
each month. The interval between the upper and lower
curves is, therefore, a measure of the mean daily range,
or the normal difference between night and day, which
is so important in its relation to the public health. Lastly,
at the upper part of the diagram are shown the mean
monthly readings of the barometer.

* See Sir John Sinclair's *Statistical Account of Scotland*, vol. vii.,
p. 247.

TEMPERATURE.

The following table gives the principal temperature-elements, the averages being calculated for the period commencing with November 1884.

	Mean of Maxima.		Mean of Minima.		Mean Temperature.	
	Strath-peffer.	Roy. Obs.	Strath-peffer.	Roy. Obs.	Strath-peffer.	Roy. Obs.
	Deg.	Deg.	Deg.	Deg.	Deg.	Deg.
January .	40·2	40·9	32·6	31·9	36·3	36·6
February .	40·7	43·0	32·3	32·7	36·5	37·7
March . .	42·4	46·5	33·0	32·5	37·7	38·9
April . .	48·9	55·3	36·6	37·3	42·7	45·4
May . .	53·9	62·8	41·2	43·2	47·5	51·5
June . .	61·5	70·8	46·6	49·2	54·0	59·1
July . .	63·0	74·9	50·2	52·7	56·6	62·8
August .	61·1	72·1	48·6	51·4	54·8	60·5
September	56·7	65·5	45·1	48·2	50·9	55·9
October .	49·3	55·2	39·9	40·8	44·6	47·6
November	44·4	48·4	36·2	38·3	40·3	43·5
December .	40·3	43·4	32·5	34·1	36·4	39·1
Year . .	...		...		44·8	48·2

The annual Mean Temperature is 44·8 degrees, or 3·4 degrees colder than that of Greenwich.* The coldest of the four years was 44·3 degrees, and the warmest was 45·7 degrees. The highest reading of the thermometer was 79·8 degrees on 18th June 1887 (the month of Jubilee fame); the lowest air-temperature was 12

---

* The mean temperature of Wick, for twenty-four years ending 1880, is 46.0 degrees; that of Dunrobin for the same period, 46·4 : that of Culloden 46·6 ; and that of Aberdeen 46·5.

degrees on 20th February 1885. The corresponding extremes at Greenwich were 92·2 degrees on 4th July 1887, and 15·5 degrees on 2nd January in the same year. The mean of the absolute lowest readings in each of the five winters is, for Strathpeffer 16·3 degrees against 18·3 degrees for the Royal Observatory. The mean of the extreme summer readings for four years is 76·2 degrees at the northern Spa against 90 degrees exactly, at Greenwich. It follows that the mean range between the extreme temperatures of summer and winter is about 12 degrees less at Strathpeffer, this difference being almost wholly due to the more temperate and equable climate of the summer.

The difference between the two stations is much more marked by day than by night. Thus the mean of the maxima for the three summer months is about 11·0 degrees greater at the Royal Observatory than at Strathpeffer; but the mean of the minima for the same period shows a difference of not more than about 2·5 degrees. How are we to explain this greater relative coolness of the northern days? The lessened *altitude* of the sun, will only account for a small fraction of the deficiency; neither can we ascribe it to an excess of *moisture* in the air, for the rainfall in summer is rather less than it is in London. Is there a *cold subsoil* retarding the development of high temperatures? Possibly so; but while the winters are so mild as they have been in recent years, this cause can only operate to a small extent. In all probability, the real cause is to be found in the cooling influence of the surrounding *sea*, coupled with the freer circulation of air upon a hillside. How marked is the contrast in the southern and midland counties of England, where an extensive surface of land is daily exposed to a summer sun, and powerfully warms the air in contact with it! *

Grouping the months into the usual meteorological **Seasons,** we have the following results :—

	Strathpeffer.	Roy. Obs.	Difference.
Winter (Dec. to February)	36·4°	37·8°	1·4°
Spring (March to May) .	42·6°	45·3°	2·7°
Summer (June to August) .	55·1°	60·8°	5·7°
Autumn (Sept. to November)	45·3°	49·0°	3·7°

It is remarkable how closely the temperatures of

* The above will doubtless explain the greater part of the difference referred to. A further query then arises, whether the *position of the instruments* may not also have a small part in the matter? At many observatories the thermometers are placed in a louvred case or screen which is freely *exposed to the sun.* The screen is often made double in order to prevent. if possible, the heat imparted to the outer case (which is very considerable) from affecting the contained thermometers. Will not an instrument thus situated record a higher temperature than if it be placed on the shady side of a building, in such a position that neither the ground beneath it, nor any wall or woodwork near it, receives any effective sunshine? The question which of those two situations better represents the *true* temperature of the air is perhaps not very easy to determine. Yet it constitutes a possible cause of considerable discrepancy—a cause which perhaps affects comparative meteorology more often than is generally supposed.

the four months, December to March, approach to one another. The latter month is only one degree warmer than February, whereas April shows an increase of five degrees over March. Temperature rises rapidly in the ensuing months,—to its maximum in July; then declines slightly in August, and more rapidly until the end of the year. The temperature of October (44·6 degrees) nearly corresponds with that of the year, and the same remark applies to the Royal Observatory, on the average of a long course of years.

The Winter Climate.

Let us glance for a moment at the general distribution of the winter temperature, as evidenced by the average of the three months December to February, at a few representative stations for the fifteen years 1871 to 1885 :—

Stornoway (Hebrides) . .	38·9
Culloden * . . .	38·0
Nairn . . .	37·7
York	38·4
Cambridge	38·7
Royal Observatory . .	39·4

Thus we perceive how small is the practical effect of the difference of latitude; for one may expect to find a

---

* Culloden is about fifteen miles south-east of Strathpeffer, and the temperature quoted above applies to the forty years 1841 to 1880.

slightly *warmer winter in the Hebrides than in York or Cambridge.*

The following are the *lowest* and highest temperatures recorded in each winter at Strathpeffer and at the Royal Observatory.*

Winter.	Strathpeffer.		Royal Observatory.	
	Lowest.	Highest.	Lowest.	Highest.
1884-5	12·0°	51·5°	22·3°	58·3°
1885-6	16·2°	54·0°	16·5°	51·5°
1886-7	17·0°	53·3°	15·4°	54·9°
1887-8	17·0°	54·0°	18·4°	54·1°
1888-9	19·5°	57·1°	18·9°	58·1°

It is interesting to note that in two winters a lower temperature was recorded at Greenwich than occurred at the northern Spa.

A question that will naturally occur to the reader is this : Can you tell me something of the comparative frequency of frosts in the winter ?   I am accustomed to distinguish three distinct varieties of frost: first, *Night frost*, where the temperature of the air at some period

---

* I regret my inability to furnish earlier records of temperature at Strathpeffer ; and the more so, as we have lately been passing through what may be termed an extensive *wave of cold*, lasting (with slight intermission) for three years, from the autumn of 1885 to the summer of 1888, and perhaps longer. Consequently the averages founded upon recent years are more or less understated.

of the twenty-four hours falls to 32 degrees or less; secondly, *Mean frost*, in which the mean temperature of the day and night, taken together, is at or below 32 degrees; thirdly (a still colder form) I have designated by the term *Entire frost*, in which the frost persists throughout the entire day, that is to say the maximum does not rise above 32 degrees.

The frequency with which *Night frosts* have occurred has varied from 35 to 59; the average of five winters (December to February) is 48, which is only slightly in excess of the corresponding numbers for the Royal Observatory. *Mean frosts* have varied from 33 in the cold winter of 1884-5 down to only 9 in that of 1888-9. Their average is about 23, and they tend to be distributed in nearly equal proportions, over the three winter months. At the Royal Observatory their numbers have varied from 20 in the winter of 1886-7, down to only 7 in that of 1884-5. Their average is 16 and nearly half of them occurred in January. Turning now to the *Entire frosts*,* we find they have varied at Strath-peffer from 2 to 13; the average of the five winters being a little over 7. The largest number in one month was also 7, and occurred twice in the successive Januaries, 1885 and 1886. At Greenwich the entire frosts varied from one to five, the average of five winters amounting to three.

A few remarks on the winter months individually

---

* An entire frost is always reckoned among the mean frosts; for it is a mean frost, and something more.

may be of interest. *December* is the period of lowest
barometer and greatest rainfall, with frequent strong
south-westerly winds. Different Decembers have varied
much in temperature : the coldest in 1886, being 32·8
degrees, and the warmest in 1888, 39·1 degrees. One
December was slightly warmer at Strathpeffer than at
Greenwich. In *January* we find the barometer not so
low as in December, and there is some abatement of the
rainfall. The temperature is curiously variable, ranging
from 32·9 degrees in 1885 to no less than 40·2 degrees
in 1889, when it was actually 0·9 deg. *warmer than
Hastings* ! It is a somewhat windy month, with occasional spells of north-easterly and north-westerly winds.
Two Januaries were respectively 1·9 deg. and 3·1 deg.
warmer than at the Royal Observatory, and in a third
the temperatures at the two stations were equal. Of
February it may be said :—

> Now shifting gales with milder influence blow,
> Cloud o'er the skies, and melt the falling snow ;
> The softened earth with fertile moisture teems,
> And, freed from icy bounds, down rush the swelling streams.

Some persons are so much in love with this month
at the Spa, that they regard it (in spite of the evidence
of the thermometers) as the first month of spring,
rather than the last of winter. The days begin rapidly
to lengthen, and the great charm of this month probably
consists in the frequent bright sunshine, which gladdens
the heart of Nature, and inspires the beholder with new
life and fresh hopes. In February the days are a little

warmer, but the nights are usually slightly colder than in January, and the mean temperature is practically unchanged. Two Februaries were rather warmer at Strathpeffer than at Greenwich; in two others the temperatures were nearly equal at both stations; but February 1885 was no less than 7·6 deg. colder than at the Royal Observatory. Curiously enough, it was by no means a cold February at Strathpeffer, but this difference was really the expression of an exceptionally warm month in the south of England. It is worth observing, that in four out of the five Februaries, the nights of Strathpeffer were warmer than those of Greenwich.

Though March is not technically a winter month, yet its temperature being only 1·2 deg. above that of February, I may perhaps be allowed to make brief allusion to it. The drier air, and clearer skies of this month admit of the not infrequent enjoyment of bright and genial sunshine. On one such day (the 18th of the month) a tortoise-shell butterfly was found sunning himself for a brief season—too big alas! for his comfort, for he had soon to learn, that one butterfly cannot make a summer. The occasional prevalence of dry easterly winds, and the freer nocturnal radiation, somewhat check the natural rise of temperature, and give to this attractive month a certain harshness, go where you will. Yet it is a striking fact that the nights of this month, (like those of January) are on the average about half a degree warmer at Strathpeffer than at Greenwich.

The comparative freedom from mist and fog, for which Strathpeffer is indebted to the friendly shelter of the western mountains, is one of the agreeable features of the winter, and together with the great purity of the air, it contributes to the remarkable brightness of the sunshine, which almost redeems the comparative shortness of the day.

Taking the last five winters severally, we may observe that the temperature varied from 35·0 to 38·5 degrees. The winter of 1884-5 was the coldest, and was 5·5 deg. lower than that at Greenwich. January was very cold and dry, its temperature being but 0·9 deg. above the freezing point.*

The winter of 1885-6 was cold and very wet, yet it was only 0·4 deg. below that of Greenwich. December was very warm and wet, with strong westerly winds. January was cold, with frequent north-easterly breezes and a rainfall of 5·1 inches—the largest amount registered in one month except in November 1888. The winter of 1886-7 set in with an unusually cold December, following upon a very warm autumn. There were twelve mean frosts in this month, and night frosts occurred twenty-four times. January was rather above the average, and February was a very warm month, with many bright sunny days: so warm and springlike

---

* It is only fair to Strathpeffer to remark that there have been nine colder Januaries at the Royal Observatory within the last seventy-four years, two of them occurring so recently as 1879 and 1881.

was it that there were only seven night frosts, and no mean frosts in this month. The temperature of the season was almost exactly equal to that of Greenwich. The winter of 1887-8 (of which the writer is able to speak from personal observation) was rather below the average, but still not more than 1·1 deg. colder than at the Royal Observatory. Its most interesting period was February. On the 2nd of this month, a slight shock of earthquake was felt in Strathpeffer. The heavy and low *rumbling* sound breaking suddenly upon the stillness of the early morning, resembled the effect produced by the passage of a row of very heavily laden waggons near the house. This sound was immediately followed by a sudden shake of the window-sashes, as though a violent gust of air had been driven against them. For the next seven days the weather was very warm and spring-like, with a little rain on each day, but the rest of the month was unusually cold and dry. The winter of 1888-9 was the warmest and driest of the series. Its mean temperature was 38·5 deg., or 0·2 deg. *warmer than at Greenwich;* and there were only nine mean frosts, against fifteen at the Royal Observatory.* It had followed a November so wet and

---

* During the winter season of ninety days (1st December 1888 to 28th February 1889) the night temperature (minimum) at Strathpeffer exceeded that of Hastings on thirty-one days; and the day temperature (maximum) on as many as thirty-seven days. Comparing the Strathpeffer readings with those of a private observer at Hertford on the north of London, Strathpeffer was warmer than Hertford on forty-seven nights and fifty-four days. The absolute

stormy that the rain-gauge was blown away (!), and there
were floods at Contin, in the neighbourhood. There
was very little snow until the 8th February, when an
almost blinding snowstorm occurred, with extensive
drifting.   The remarkably springlike character of the
season—the warm air and brilliant sun, acting upon a soil
already fertilized by the November rains,—forced vegeta-
tion into early growth.   Primroses were out in December,
a bouquet of violets, stock and polyanthus was gathered
in my brother's garden early in January, and shortly
afterwards the japonica, yellow jasmine, snowdrops,
and even roses, were found blooming out of doors.

RAINFALL.

This is a familiar and well-worn theme.   There is no
feature of climate more readily recognized or more
attentively scanned, even by the untrained observer,
than the rainfall, and none that presents more striking
variations in different parts of our Islands.

The area of lowest rainfall, varying in amount from
22·5 to 25·0 inches *per annum*, is stated by Mr. Buchan,
to extend "from the Humber to the estuary of the
Thames, exclusive of the higher grounds of Lincoln and
Norfolk, where the average rainfall exceeds twenty-five
inches."   On the other hand, the heaviest falls occur

---

highest and lowest temperatures recorded at the three stations
during the same period were : *Maxima*, Strathpeffer 57·1, Hastings
54·8, Hertford 54·5. *Minima*, Hastings 22, Strathpeffer 19·4,
Hertford 12.

where the south-west winds are opposed in their course
by the high mountain masses of the northern Highlands,
of the Lake District of Cumberland, and of North and
South Wales. The wettest place in Scotland appears to
be Glencroe in Argyle, where the mean of six years,
ending in 1870 was 128·50 inches. Even this, however,
sinks into relative insignificance compared with The
Stye, in Cumberland, reputed to be the wettest place in
the three kingdoms, where the rainfall for twelve years
was at the rate of fifteen and a half *feet* per annum.

Stations.	Years.	Date.	Inches.
Sandwick (Orkneys)	24	1860-83	37·23
Strome Ferry	12	1872-83	65·30
Dunrobin (Sutherlandshire)	24	1860-83	30·08
Invergordon	19	1865-83	27·26
Dingwall	17	1865-81	27·50
Strathpeffer Spa	4	1885-88	**28·91**
Culloden (Inverness)	24	1860-83	26·17
Acharaidh (Nairn)	21	1863-83	23·92
Edinburgh	24	1860-83	28·31
Glasgow	24	1860-83	43·00
Grasmere	18	1866-83	82·80
The Stye (Cumberland)	12	1865-69 1872 1878-83	185·96
Harrogate	20	1861-80	33·17
Buxton	15	1866-80	57·14
Matlock	17	1867-83	39·71
Bath	24	1860-83	33·58
Beddgelert (Carnarvon)	20	1860-79	115·08
Torquay	20	1864-83	38·36
Ventnor	24	1860-83	30·52
Brighton	22	1862-83	29·04
Hastings	24	1860-83	29·01
Tunbridge	24	1860-83	28·80
Margate	20	1864-83	24·00
Royal Observatory (Greenwich)	71	1815-85	25·19

The preceding table (p. 29) gives a comparative view of the annual rainfall at several different stations, with the number of years upon which the averages have been calculated.

Starting from the south-east of England, where the rainfall is least, we observe that in travelling westwards or northwards, there is a marked increase of precipitation. Again, how striking is the contrast between the eastern and western coasts of Scotland! We see that while the rainfall of Edinburgh and Strathpeffer is about 28 inches, and that of Dunrobin 30 inches ; Glasgow has an annual fall of 43 inches, and Strome Ferry of 65 inches *per annum.*

The *seasonable distribution* of the rainfall, and the number of *rainy days* on the average of four to five years, are given on p. 31.*

The last four years seem to have been alternately dry and wet, the driest year (1887) having 26·36 inches of rain, and the wettest one (1886) amounting to 31·16 inches. If we may rely upon so short an average, it appears that 52 *per cent* of the annual rainfall occurs in the five months, October to February. The lion's share falls to December and November. The months with the

---

* A fall of at least one-hundredth of an inch of rain (or its equivalent in snow) is understood to constitute a "rainy day." But as it often happens that the rain falls *in the night*, leaving the hours of daylight clear, we have carefully to distinguish between the technical and the popular acceptation of this somewhat misleading term.

lowest average rainfall appear to be the alternate ones,
April, June, and August—*June being, so far, the driest
period of the year.* As in London, so at Strathpeffer,
there is a distinct tendency to increased precipitation in
July, which subsides in the two following months, and is
thus marked off from the autumnal rainy period. As was

	Mean Rainfall at Strathpeffer.	Mean number of Rainy Days.
	Inches.	
January . .	2·71	17
February . .	2·57	17
March . .	1·96	14
April . . .	1·68	13
May . . .	2·08	18
June . . .	1·52	12
July . . .	2·59	18
August . .	1·67	15
September . .	2·45	17
October . .	2·76	17
November . .	3·35	17
December . .	3·67	19
Year	28·91	198

shrewdly observed long ago, by Luke Howard, the father
of Modern Meteorology, the *æstival* rains are of different
origin and character from the *autumnal.* The former
occur in the hottest part of the year, when we partake
in slight degree "in the operation of the same causes
which produce the heavy tropical rains." We have a
relatively high barometer; the air is comparatively clear

and calm; there are light and variable breezes, and the
rain is precipitated in the more elevated regions and
falls through relatively dry air.   The autumnal rains, on
the other hand, are due to the prevailing warm south-
westerly current, which gathers moisture as it sweeps
over the Atlantic, to discharge it upon our colder
latitudes.   Hence there is, not only frequent rainfall, but
a prevailing "turbidity" or moistness of the atmosphere,
in those places that have not the advantage, possessed
by Strathpeffer, of a screen of mountains to windward.

The rainfall measured in one month amounted to five
inches or upwards on three occasions—in January, July,
and November; the *wettest month* in the four years and
a half being November 1888, when 5·2 inches were
registered.   On the other hand, the monthly rainfall fell
short of one inch on six occasions, once namely, in each
of the six months from March to August.   The driest
month of the series was June 1887, when the amount was
exactly half an inch.   The months wherein the amount
of rain varies least from year to year, appear to be
March, April, and October; whilst July, November, and
January are those wherein the greatest fluctuation is
perceptible.   Thus the difference between the driest
and the wettest March was 1·2 inch, but between the
driest and the wettest July the difference was no less
than 4·3 inches.

Finally, the Strathpeffer observations inform us that
the four months, May to August, are, as will be seen
from the diagram, drier there than at London.

The barometric curve, represented in the diagram just referred to, shows that, on the limited average of between four and five years, there is a distinct maximum in June, which is also the driest month. The mercury usually falls somewhat in July; the mean monthly readings then remain fairly level for the next two months, after which they fall quickly to their lowest value in December, which is the wettest month. A partial recovery of pressure takes place in January and February; the mean values continue without much change throughout the spring, and then rise sharply, to return to the maximum in June. The difference between the average height of the barometer in this month and in December is 0·42 inch. The months in which there is least variation from year to year in the mean readings are August, April and June, which also happen to be the three dry months. Those in which the annual variation is greatest are January, February and September.

The mean monthly *range* of the barometer is considerably greater in every month than is the case in London, and this is just what we should expect from its more exposed situation. At both places the range is greatest from November to January, and is least in June and July. It seems to be a general rule that a wide range accompanies low pressure, and a small

3

range—in other words, greater *steadiness*—is associated with high readings of the barometer.

In conclusion, so far as our experience at present extends, Strathpeffer may be said to enjoy a temperate and fairly equable climate, combining the advantages of marine and mountain situation, at the same time that it is to a large extent free from the drawbacks that accompany a situation too exclusively of one kind or the other.

The *Summers* are decidedly cooler than in the south of England, but they are bright, breezy, and dry, especially in June and August. The long days invite to an open-air life and vigorous exercise, which can be enjoyed without the enervating effect of the heat that is found so trying in many parts of England and on the Continent. There is also the advantage of a pure ozoniferous mountain air.

We have seen that the *Winters* are on the average a little colder than in the neighbourhood of London, but that the nights at least are often warmer. Moreover, the days are not spoiled by the fogs and mists so often met with in the south of England ; and the rain-clouds have a knack of clearing off readily, so that frequent spells of bright sunshine, such as are hardly known in London, make walking a delight, even though the ground may be carpeted with crisp snow.

In the present day when Climate has rightly assumed such a prominent place in medical treatment, the

Meteorology of Health Resorts is a study of no slight importance. Much no doubt remains to be done to determine the influence of the several factors, singly and in combination. Only prolonged observation and careful comparison suffice to establish trustworthy conclusions. Here as elsewhere, the truth applies which was expressed in the shrewd saying of old—

Nil sine magno
Musa labore dedit mortalibus.

CHAPTER III.

THE Sulphur Springs of Strathpeffer belong to the class of *Cold Sulphur Waters*, a class particularly well represented in Great Britain; and among others by Harrogate in England, Llandrindod and Llanwrtyd in Wales, Lisdunvarna and Lucan in Ireland, and by Moffat in the south and Strathpeffer in the north of Scotland. Chalybeates, by a happy circumstance, are very apt to occur in the neighbourhood of such springs, and Strathpeffer makes no exception to the rule.* On the Continent of Europe, in addition to the cold sulphur, there are numerous warm, or *Thermal, Sulphur Waters*, but these, as we shall presently see, are for the most part very weak in the sulphur elements.

In this large class of waters, whether warm or cold, the greater portion of sulphur is chemically united with hydrogen gas, forming the well-known compound, *hydric sulphide*, or Sulphuretted Hydrogen—the gas which gives to such waters not only their peculiar taste and

---

* The Chalybeate, or Iron. Wells of Strathpeffer Spa are described in a separate chapter.

odour, but also very much of their efficacy. A second combination of sulphur is with metals, as *alkaline sulphides*; and, lastly, there exists in some of these springs more or less of the same element in a *free* or *suspended* state. In the Strathpeffer Wells sulphur occurs *in all three forms*—so richly as to make them in point of strength, as in geographical position, nearly at the head of British sulphur springs.

The name "*Harrogate of the Highlands*," which the northern Spa has sometimes received, is in many points an accurate designation. The waters of Harrogate are, it is true, stronger in their large *saline* constituent, chiefly consisting of chloride of sodium or common salt, the ingredient which gives them their bitter taste and which is nearly absent from the Strathpeffer Springs. But the more thoroughly the two waters are known (and Harrogate has the advantage of more numerous and modern analyses), the more nearly they are found to approximate in what are, without doubt, their most valuable ingredients, namely the *Sulphur* compounds.

The minute comparison of different mineral waters of the same class, although interesting, is a matter of no little difficulty, and scarcely perhaps of commensurate importance. The chances of error are numerous. Analyses by different chemists—separated in point of time by many years, following, therefore, in all probability different methods of determination, subject also to differences arising from the season of the year in which the examinations were made, and whether conducted upon the spot or upon bottled waters in a laboratory at a distance—render a just comparison hopeless in many cases, more particularly where gases are concerned.

An example of the peculiar difficulties attending these comparisons may be found in the manual of the late Dr. Manson.* Dr. Manson, with the published analyses before him, sought to compare the Strong Well at Strathpeffer with the strongest waters of Harrogate. For the contents of the former he had the high authority of Dr. Murray Thomson (1857), for those of Harrogate that of Professor Hoffman (1853). From the analyses of these chemists it followed that the Scottish water contained *sulphuretted hydrogen* (hydric sulphide) in more than twice the quantity found at Harrogate, although falling considerably short of Harrogate in *alkaline sulphides.* So matters stood until 1875, when Dr. Thorpe showed, by a more perfect method, that the old sulphur spring at the English Spa was considerably richer in the hydric sulphide than had been supposed by former analysts; that in fact it approached, in this respect, much more nearly to the Strong Well of Strathpeffer; having, on Dr. Thorpe's showing, 10·16 cubic inches of this gas to the gallon, as compared with 11·26 cubic inches (Thomson) at the latter place. Further as respects alkaline sulphides, the *new analysis* continued to show for the Harrogate water a superiority over the *old analysis* at the sister Spa, although, once more, not to the extent that had been supposed.

---

* *Strathpeffer Spa*, 5th ed., p. 12.

In the face of such unexpected discoveries it may be permitted to doubt whether the comparison has reached its final stage, even yet ; but, in the meantime it remains true, in Dr. Manson's words, that the " Strathpeffer Strong Well contains the largest quantity of sulphuretted hydrogen in any known spring in Great Britain ;" whilst, so far, the palm for the alkaline (sodium) combination of sulphur remains, among British Spas, with Harrogate. It is not, however, wonderful that in waters containing large quantities of salt (chloride of sodium), as at Harrogate, the sulphide of the same metal should be found more abundantly than in waters almost devoid of this salt. As regards the hydric sulphide, in which the Strathpeffer springs are by common consent pre-eminently rich, much larger proportions than those quoted above have been noted by competent observers at Strathpeffer, particularly in the colder months ; but to this, reference will again be made.

After all, the advantages of analysis by the most approved and trustworthy methods, with every regard to season and other natural conditions, are to be prized far more in the interests of science than from any anxiety to excel Home Spas, associated in a common service. On the other hand, to show that English, Scotch, and Irish Mineral Waters are many of them equal in chemical and medicinal properties to the much praised springs of France and Germany, may be regarded as a service not only to truth but to country.

In the numerous analyses of the Continental waters belonging to this class the *sulphur element* is sometimes given as cubic inches of the gas, and sometimes as grains *per* gallon of sulphides or of the element sulphur itself. As we shall afterwards have occasion to note, no valid distinction can, for medicinal purposes, be drawn between the gaseous (hydric) and the alkaline (sodium) sulphide; or, if there be any, it would seem to be in favour of the more volatile compound. The two forms of sulphide may therefore, for practical purposes, be considered as one. In the following table the author has grouped some of the more important Continental sulphur springs, both cold and thermal. The figures represent the total weight both of sulphuretted hydrogen and of alkaline sulphides in grains per gallon.*

Combined Alkaline and Hydric Sulphide.

	Grains per gallon.
(1) Cold Sulphur Waters—	
[Strathpeffer .	6·17]
Eillsen . . .	6·03
Nenndorf . .	4·53
Weilbach	0·61

* It is exceedingly difficult to be entirely accurate in a comparison of this kind; and no great importance must be attached to the smaller differences. The results are calculated on a careful comparison of various published analyses. See *Curative Effects of Baths and Waters*, Dr. Braun; *Baths and Wells of Europe*, J. Macpherson M.D.; *Watering Places of Germany*, Dr. Gutmann; *Harrogate and its Waters*, Geo. Oliver M.D.; *Mineral Waters of Aix-les-Bains*, Dr. Blanc; *etc.*

(2) Thermal Sulphur Waters—

Luchon . . .	3·90
Barèges . . .	. 3·60
Aix-la-Chapelle	. . 2·65
Cauterets	. . 2·10
St. Sauveur .	. 1·47
Aix-les-Bains . .	. 0·57
Eaux Bonnes . .	0·57
Eaux Chaudes	0·50

As a class the Cold Sulphur Waters are far stronger than the Thermal or Warm Waters; an observation which agrees with the familiar effect of heat in dissipating and breaking up the combination of sulphides. The famous Pyrenean waters, Luchon and Barèges, are *for thermals* uncommonly rich in these ingredients, the former containing nearly two-thirds the proportion of the Strong Well at the Scottish Spa.

Three sulphur waters are at present drunk at Strathpeffer. Of these, the Strong (or New) Well and the Old Well rise directly under the Pump Room floor from fissures in the slaty rock, whilst the Upper Well has been conveyed thither through ebonite tubes from its source on a higher level one hundred yards distant. All are, therefore, now served under one roof. These waters have been repeatedly examined by experts. The following table is compiled from the latest analyses, made in 1857 by Dr. Murray Thomson, of Edinburgh :—

Synopsis of Analysis of the Strathpeffer Sulphur Waters.
IN IMPERIAL GALLON.*

	STRONG WELL.	OLD WELL.	UPPER WELL.
I. SOLIDS.	Grains.	Grains.	Grains.
Sulphate of Lime . . .	50·92	18·89	23·43
Carbonate of Lime . .	14·88	7·43	6·24
Phosphate of Lime and Magnesia	0·50	0·43	...
Sulphate of Magnesia . .	31·08	...	39·18
Carbonate of Magnesia . .	traces	1·09	1·78
Sulphate of Soda . . .	5·86	2·47	9·87
Sulphuret of Sodium . .	0·53	0·78	0·12
Sulphuret of Potassium . .	1·30	...	0·89
Silica	2·14	0·77	3·06
Organic Matters . . .	1·02	2·66	2·35
Sulphur in Suspension . .	4·07	2·47	1·84
Chlorine	traces	...	...
Chloride of Sodium . . .	...	4·60	4·54
Potass Salts	...	traces	...
Sulphide of Iron . . .	...	...	1·08
	112·30	41·59	94·38
II. GASES.			
Sulphuretted Hydrogen . .	4·34	1·60	1·21
The same in cubic inches .	11·26	4·01	3·03
Carbonic Acid—undetermined .			

In respect to the Strong Well, Dr. Thomson remarks :—

"The water had no action on either red or blue
litmus paper exposed to its action for more than an
hour. When a delicate thermometer was plunged into

---

* Equal to 160 fluid ounces; 70,000 grains, in weight; and 277
cubic inches by volume.

the cistern, and allowed to remain ten minutes, it showed a temperature of 55 degs. Fahr., the temperature of the atmosphere at the same time being 59 degs.

"The amount of sulphuretted hydrogen was twice determined in September 1857, and once again in September 1859. On these trials the quantities given were respectively 4·48, 4·64, and 4·00 grains of this gas in a gallon. The mean of these numbers is 4·34, which, converted into cubic inches, gives 11·26 as the volume of sulphuretted hydrogen in an imperial gallon. The qualitative analysis showed the presence of—Base: lime, magnesia, potass, soda, trace of iron. Acids: sulphuric, carbonic, phosphoric, hydrosulphuric, silicic, and sulphur. Besides these there was present a very small amount of organic matter.

"The specific gravity of the water at 60 degs. is 1002·46.

" I may also add that this water can retain for a long time a good deal of its sulphuretted hydrogen gas. A sealed bottle opened twenty days after my visit to Strathpeffer contained this gas in quantity at the rate of 2·08 grains in a gallon, or nearly one-half of what it had at the Well."

In 1860, samples of the water were sent to London for examination by Dr. Medlock. He found of sulphuretted hydrogen, in the Old Well 2·33 inches, in the Strong Well 5·61 inches, and in the Upper Well about 9 cubic inches; and expressed the opinion that the quantity would be found very much larger " if the gas analysis were made on the spot." Indeed, very much larger quantities of the sulphur gas had been recorded in 1829 by a Dr. Henderson in Aberdeen, and subsequently by the late Dr. Thompson of Glasgow, who found in the Upper Well as much as 26 cubic inches per gallon.

The last systematic observations are recorded in his treatise by the late Dr. Manson. * They were made by him in the winter of 1882-3, when the sulphureous impregnation, owing to the coldness of the air, was at its highest. He says:—"On the morning of November 7th, 1882, with the barometer at 29·4 and the thermometer at 42 degs. Fahr., and after strong frost the previous night, the writer found by a correct process the quantities of sulphuretted hydrogen in the respective springs to be—16·1 cubic inches to the gallon in the Strong Well, 20·5 in the Upper Well, and 7·5 in the Old Well. On examining again by the very same process on the morning of April 26th, 1883, with the barometer at 29·2 and the thermometer at 43 degs. Fahr., and after a cold night, the respective quantities were : for the Strong Well 22·7, for the Upper Well 27·1, for the Old Well 7·3, cubic inches to the gallon." Dr. Manson further makes the practical observation : "*If, therefore, it be desired to have as much of the sulphur gas as possible, then the colder time of the year, and* ESPECIALLY THE SPRING, *is best for taking the water.*" The present writer is well able to corroborate his predecessor's conclusion upon this point.

---

* *Op. cit.,* p. 16.

It is to be noted that the sulphur very readily breaks away from its combination with hydrogen, or with alkaline metals. Heat, agitation, or exposure to the air, soon bring about this decomposition. It is, therefore, very advisable to "take the waters" fresh from the Well. No doubt, the very instability of the constituents renders their action in the system more active and immediate. The older chemists were of opinion that this loosely combined attachment of the sulphur and the hydrogen was altogether special to natural mineral waters. The yellowish crust, or "cream," of free sulphur, which covers the wells, if exposed to the air, was at one time much sought after by drinkers, on account of its supposed special efficacy. The efficacy of the element in the loose combination above referred to is, however, far greater.

The rock out of which the sulphur waters of Strathpeffer flow, and from which, in the course of long subterranean travel, they no doubt derive their chemical properties, has been analyzed by J. McG. Ross, Esq., of Alness. The following are his results :—

	per cent.
Bituminous Organic Matter, and Water .	4·8
Sulphate of Lime . . .	10·3
Carbonate of Lime	45·0
Carbonate of Magnesia . . .	19·1
Carbonate of Iron . . .	1·6
Insoluble (Silicates, etc.) . .	18·8
	99·6

CHAPTER IV.

THE ancient practice of treating disease by mineral waters gains rather than loses support with the advance of medical science. The theory, which is altogether a different matter, may be changed in this or disproved in that particular; some of the older pretensions, not more extravagant here than in any other department of bygone treatment, may fall to the ground; but the practice itself survives, and founds itself more and more surely with the lapse of time, upon a permanent scientific basis.

The prime virtue of natural waters as a remedy is this, that they hold their constituents *in a state the most favourable to absorption.* That is no slight title to favour. When it is considered that in many or most disorders the function of absorption is itself deranged, how important it becomes that the curative agent should be presented in the most acceptable mode. It is the province of the physician not only to give the right remedy, but *to get it into the body*, and this mineral waters often enable him to do.

Upon what basis are these brief statements founded ? It is obvious in the first place, that waters of all kinds hold all their contents *in solution.* That is of itself favourable to absorption ; for, indeed, solution is the needful preliminary to absorption, so important that to it the whole work of digestion is devoted. When matters are dissolved, the component particles are separated, and are therefore more free to act upon any surface with which they come in contact. The active operation of the particles in animals and plants is further intensified, in the case of watery solutions by the penetrating power of the fluid in which they are dissolved ; and not only by its powers of mechanical penetration, but also by the chemical affinity of water for the living tissues. A watery solution may be of any proportion, from the point of saturation (strongest possible solution) to the vanishing point (weakest possible). In the case of all the natural waters (for internal use), it will be found that the solution is, as to strength, a long way below the point of saturation.

Perfect solution of their contents is the first notable characteristic ; *free dilution* is the second. One result of dilution is to diminish the local activity of any substance in such a way as often to remove altogether a certain class of effects—for example caustic or astringent actions,—which may be described as the primary local effects of the substance in question. These actions are often antagonistic to absorption, and being removed by dilution, absorption takes place. An opportunity is then given for the development of a new series of effects, secondary effects both local and in the system at large—for whatever of this kind the remedial agent is competent to produce. Its first difficulty is to pass the gates of Absorption. And here it is almost invariably resisted and excluded, unless accompanied by a proper degree of dilution, or, to use a common metaphor, unless it rides in a capacious watery vehicle.

It is therefore clear in the next place, that the therapeutic effect of a mineral water is compound, being in part assignable to the water of dilution, and in part to the particular constituents dissolved in it. When the bulk imbibed does not exceed the normal allowance of water in health the first element may be neglected. On the other hand it is quite usual for persons under Spa treatment to drink twice, or three or four times, their normal allowance of fluid, or even much more ; and therefore the effect of an excess of water must not be lost sight of.

As this question of the internal use of water thus lies at the threshold of any inquiry into the use of *mineral* waters, it must be here briefly adverted to. Pure water, when carried into the stomach, very soon leaves that organ. It is conveyed away by the veins, and yet it has no appreciable effect in increasing the fluid contents of the blood. The pulse-frequency may be somewhat lowered and the blood pressure slightly raised. The imbibed water then rapidly distributes itself among the tissues of the body, and stimulates the circulation of the fluids. The *washing-out* of the tissues, always more or less in process, is thus promoted; and naturally there is an augmented removal of waste matter, and of water itself, by the kidneys and by the skin. For these reasons water-drinking is recommended when it is desired, by irrigation of the tissues, to wash away waste matter or poison, or to promote the absorption of deposits and exudations. An abundant use of hot water, or cold, in some form or another, is the main factor of medical treatment in many conditions of chronic disorder, where these ends are in view. For precisely the same purpose many such cases frequent the mineral Spas, where the use of water may be had, combined with every circumstance of advantage to health, in climate, diet, and simplicity of life. On the contrary, no one should come for treatment to mineral waters in whose case, from any cause, the free use of fluids is inadvisable. So much may be affirmed of the watery vehicle, the omnipresent element which permeates Nature in such a manner that even in human bodies there is nearly sixty *per cent.* by weight of it. In the mineral spring, water preponderates to a still greater extent, to such an extent indeed, that some are inclined —reacting too violently from the bad science of the past - - to neglect entirely what they regard as the " insignificant proportion " of the dissolved ingredients.

Dismissing, then, the vehicle, what can be safely and generally said of the ingredients? Beyond the facts already observed, that they are presented in a state of

4

solution and in a high degree of dilution, we have the remarkable circumstance pointed out by Dr. Saunders,* that some of them occur in a form or composition, not available elsewhere than in mineral springs. For example, carbonated iron springs, like the Strathpeffer chalybeate (*see* Chap. VI.) hold in solution Carbonate of Iron ; and in no other form can Carbonate of Iron be presented *in solution* for absorption. Again, sulphuretted hydrogen, apart from sulphur waters, is not employed in medicine. It is true that reliance is placed on the fact that in the ordinary administration of sulphur in bulk chemical changes take place *in the body*, by which sulphuretted hydrogen is produced, and so enabled to exercise its effect upon the tissues. But this artificial generation of the gas takes place, for the most part, in the intestines, and not in the stomach where absorption of fluids and gases is most active. So that it remains true that sulphur waters stand alone in the possession and effective use of a remedy, not in the same form employed in medicine. This is an important circumstance. The tissue effects (if such a phrase may be allowed), or the alterative effects, of sulphur are, as will presently be noticed, of a special and valuable character; but to obtain these effects (whatever they are), by appropriate doses frequently repeated, it is needful in the present state of science to have recourse to Sulphur Waters.

Another character of the ingredient is that it is pre-

* *Treatise on Mineral Waters*, by William Saunders, M.D., F.R.S., F.R.C.P., 1805.

sented in comparatively small doses. Salines, Iron,
Sulphur are ordinarily dispensed and taken in bulks
vastly exceeding their mixture in the laboratory of
nature. How much of the large dose may be needful,
as above hinted, to compensate for defective absorption ?
To the use of iron it is particularly applicable that the
small dose in an acceptable form is more effective than
a much larger dose in another form. Again, the activity
of the ingredient and the effect of the dose are increased,
within certain limits, by dilution, for thereby "it is
diffused equally over the extensive surface of the
stomach, and is enabled to act all at once in the most
advantageous manner possible."* Further, when, as in
the case of sulphur waters, the chief ingredient is a gas,
it is futile to employ the scale of dosage applicable to
solid and liquid matters, as will shortly appear more
particularly. Finally, the question of doses is after all
in these days very much a matter of opinion, and in
which the mode and circumstances of administration—
whether, for example, received upon an empty stomach
—must be taken into account.†

According to the latest analyses ‡ the *Strong*, or *New*,

* Dr. Saunders, *loc. cit.*

† Mr. Darwin, experimenting by dosage of certain plants, brought
a quantity of phosphate of ammonia nearly equal to a one-twenty-
millionth part of a grain into *effective contact* with a sensitive
structure, the gland upon the leaf of a sundew. The tentacle moved
upon this infinitesimal stimulation : the dose produced its effect.—
Insectivorous Plants.

‡ Dr. Murray Thomson. 1857.

Well at Strathpeffer contains eleven and a quarter cubic inches of sulphuretted hydrogen gas in the imperial gallon, in addition to about two grains of alkaline sulphide. The latter may be accepted, medicinally, as equivalent to an additional portion of the gas.* It does not appear that any valid therapeutic distinction can be drawn between the alkaline and the hydric sulphide. Taken together, these sulphur compounds are the prime ingredients of the Strathpeffer water. The presence of a small quantity of gypsum and of sulphate of magnesia, in varying proportions in the different wells, may, or may not, appreciably modify the special effect of the sulphide. It is, however, an experimental fact that in many cases, whilst the *Strong Well* is not tolerated, the *Upper Well* can be easily digested ; and there are a few examples of the reverse. This often-noted difference is of an undoubted value, and must clearly depend on the secondary ingredients. At Strathpeffer there is only a faint trace of common salt, or chloride of sodium (four grains and a half in the Upper Well). In this feature lies the great distinction, medicinally, between these waters and those of Harrogate. At Harrogate the special effects of the sulphur are powerfully modified by the presence of nearly nine hundred grains of this salt per gallon (Royal Pump Room).

Whilst, therefore, the English water is a bitter or

---

* "Sulphurets only produce an effect by their oxidation and partial transformation into sulphuretted hydrogen."—*Curative Effects of Baths and Waters*, p. 413 : Dr. Braun.

purging sulphur, that of the Highland Spa is by comparison a pure or simple sulphur water. The effects
produced are mainly those of the sulphur elements, and
when purging is desired salines are added.

It remains to examine in some further detail these
sulphur elements—the prime ingredient of the Strathpeffer waters. It is well known that the physical properties of gases are peculiarly favourable to absorption.
In the gaseous state of matter, the forces of cohesion
have been overcome by *repulsion*, and the particles are in
a state of the most perfect *mobility*, tending to fly off in
every direction. Gases also possess a high penetrating
power, or power of *diffusion* ; and in addition, a peculiar
attraction for the surfaces of solid and liquid bodies, in
virtue of which these surfaces are able to absorb them
to a greater or less extent. Sulphuretted hydrogen gas
exhibits in a high degree all these physical properties
The property of absorption is particularly well marked,
sulphuretted hydrogen being in this respect considerably more active than carbonic acid, and very much
more so than elementary oxygen and hydrogen. It is
further an inflammable gas and freely soluble in
water,* from which however it is readily liberated,

---

* Water at ordinary temperature will dissolve a little more than
three times its own volume of Sulphuretted Hydrogen. In the
Strathpeffer "Strong Well" (analysis 1857) the strength is one
volume in twenty-four of water, that is to say one seventy-ninth of
full saturation. It is doubtful whether a stronger impregnation than
this would be generally tolerated by the stomach.

especially on agitation or by the application of heat.
Hence when sulphur waters are taken into the stomach,
the medicinal gas is applied to the entire absorbent
surface of that cavity.

Taken in large doses, by the rapid process of *dry in-
halation*, sulphuretted hydrogen is a poison, destroying
life by its destructive action on the tissues, but particularly on the blood. In moderate doses of the watery
solution by the stomach, it is freely absorbed ; and,
whilst producing no immediate or obvious effect on the
blood, exerts both upon it and upon the tissues a slow
" alterative " action. This shows itself in a modification
of the processes of growth, particularly in the joints and
in the skin. The influence on the nutrition of the skin
will be referred to in the chapter on Baths. It is perhaps worthy of remark that the active absorption and
diffusibility of this gas in the body, is indicated by the
blackening of silver articles worn next the skin, whilst
the waters are being taken internally.

The effects of sulphur waters have been carefully
studied at Weilbach in Germany.* At Strathpeffer,
observations extending over a much shorter time would
seem to correspond very nearly with those of the German
observers.† It is found that in the majority of cases the
waters are not in themselves aperient, but rather the

---

* Sulphuretted hydrogen occurs in the Weilbach Waters in the
proportion of 1·6 cubic inches per gallon, just one seventh part of
the strength of the Strathpeffer " Strong Well." (11·26 inches).

† Dr. Braun, *op. cit.*, p. 414.

contrary. Their main effect is, therefore, not to be attributed to increased intestinal action. In the stomach, particularly at the commencement of treatment they sometimes "lie heavily," and do not produce the refreshing effect of carbonated waters. In course of time however, as the stomach becomes habituated to their presence, this passes off, and a sense of strong hunger is felt after their use, generally combined with a greatly increased power of digestion.

These are the effects in the stomach. The influence exerted by sulphur water on the liver is equally important. It is difficult, if not impossible, to frame a satisfactory theory to account for all the effects produced : but the fact is accepted that in cases of enlarged liver the administration of sulphur very generally reduces the enlargement, and brings about a healthier condition, not only in the functions of the liver, but in the closely related function of the disposal of waste. For, a circulation loaded with waste products is not without a deleterious effect on the liver.

In what manner sulphur exerts an alterative influence in the blood and tissues we do not know. The work is done in secret, but the results appear openly, in counteracting perverted modes of nutrition in the digestive organs, joints, or skin. Moreover sulphur water stimulates the functions of the kidney. A markedly diuretic effect—much more than the water of dilution is competent to account for—was noticed at Strathpeffer by the earliest observers, and hence cases of disordered kidney action and of gravel have always been frequent at the Spa.   Good service is certainly done in washing away gouty obstructions and deposits from these organs, as well as other kinds of gravelly concretion.

Having thus examined the different medicinal effects of sulphur waters, both in virtue of their water and of their sulphur, from a general point of view ; it remains to state some particular indications for the use of the sulphur waters of Strathpeffer.

Following the order above adopted, there are, in the first place affections of the *stomach.*   Among these, perhaps the *catarrhal form of dyspepsia* is most amenable to these waters.   In this affection the catarrh usually extends beyond the area of the stomach itself.   The mucous membrane is no doubt congested and covered with a tenacious layer, and there is on this account a more or less widespread defect or deficiency in the power of absorption.   It is dangerous to theorize, and it will be prudent to refrain from the attempt to describe the *mode by which* the persevering use of the Strathpeffer sulphur water rectifies the disordered condition of the membrane.   When the dyspepsia is accompanied by *constipation,* the use of the Upper Well in the morning is often sufficient to correct it : but where a more powerful dose is required, a teaspoonful or more of one of the salines is commonly taken, dissolved in the early morning draught of the Spa water.   There are also cases in which, as at Harrogate, a smart dose is advisable at the commencement of the treatment.   The "*tropical*" or "*Indian*" *liver* (*see* Case X.) is benefited at many Spas, and notably by sulphur waters. Many excellent results have been obtained at Strathpeffer. The large, congested, and perhaps tender, liver is reduced in size ; and, what is exceedingly important, the system is cleared of the waste matter, which in such disorders is almost always present in great excess. The treatment is often aided by Douche Baths and Massage. But it cannot be expected to avail (and the neglect of this rule may account for some disappointments) unless there be observed a due conformity with the moderated diet and regimen of the Health Resort.

Connected with the last, is the condition of fulness and *plethora* (especially of the liver and abdominal organs) which results in our own country from the combination of an overstimulating diet with a sedentary life. Here also, important districts of the circulation are both sluggish and loaded, and there is imperfect elimination of waste, causing perhaps distressing symptons of "*biliousness*" and nervous depression. In this class also, sulphur water, the first daily dose of which may suitably be taken *hot*, is (with regimen) a most successful treatment. The same may be said of *jaundice*, whether due to the presence of gallstones, or to catarrh (Case XI.). The author has known two cases in which jaundice (from the first cause) *supervened* in the course of Sulphur Water Treatment ; but the risk of this contingency is not such as to forbid the use of treatment that is both preventive and curative in a remarkable degree.

Intimately related both to disorder of the liver and to plethora there is, in the next place, a large group of cases in which the circulation and tissues are burdened, not only by an excess of waste, but by an excess of *acid material*. But here the normal processes of tissue change are perverted, and the kidneys are also very generally at fault. Short of true *gout*, which is the most characteristic member of this group, there are varieties of *acidity*, differing according to the region in which the predominant effects are manifested. Assuming that no acute disease is present, and that there is nothing to make the administration of fluids inadvisable, such cases are certain to benefit by Sulphur Water Treatment. Differing in every minor point, these all agree in owning both one cause and one mode of cure.

For the Sulphur Treatment as applied to ordinary gout reference may be made to Cases III. and VI. The author's experience inclines him more and more to believe that, although with care it may be used very soon after the acute attack, it is less beneficial then than after a considerable interval has elapsed. Even after an interval, threatening pains often return in the affected parts, when the waters have been taken for a few days : which may be taken as an indication of the influence they exert on the seat of the disease. Sulphur waters are an invaluable *preventive* of gout ; and according to this view, succeed *best* in removing the cause when the periodical effect is in comparative abeyance. Being also essentially radical in their operation, they offer a good

prospect of permanent cure. But it is to be remembered
that the process of arresting a constitutional error is
above all things, gradual, and needs the persevering
and repeated use of the remedy. And not only so, but
also a religious avoidance of all the original causes of
mischief.

A later stage in these disordered or perverted processes is presented in the persons of those who have had
gouty symptoms for many years, and now labour under
some more serious organic malady. Without unduly
enlarging on a purely medical question, it may be well
to state that in such cases the greatest caution is needful
in the use of Mineral Waters and Baths. Yet curious to
relate, if ample time be allowed, some of the most
striking successes are met with under these very un-
promising conditions of the system. The mode in which,
for such patients, Sulphur and Chalybeate Treatment can
be beneficially employed—sometimes one alone, and
sometimes both in succession—is illustrated in the
narrative of Cases IV. and V.

Among affections of the kidneys, not included in the
last group, cases of simple acid concretion do well
at Strathpeffer. In advanced degenerative disease sulphur waters are quite inappropriate; but, as will appear
in a later chapter, Chalybeate Treatment may answer
remarkably well.

Stiff limbs and mineral waters have always been
associated, both by medical and popular prescription.
Therefore all much-frequented Spas will usually exhibit,

among other conditions, every gradation from true gout in the joints to true rheumatism. With regard to these numerous and interesting intermediate cases, observation inclines the author to be more sanguine of improvement in those in which a gouty factor can be traced. At the same time, many cases of simple *chronic rheumatism* certainly do well, and the late Dr. Manson, from a long experience, always strongly recommended the waters, not only for Rheumatism, but for *scrofulous affections* of the bones and joints.

There is another group of joint affections, rapid in onset and disastrous in effects, which is remarkably connected with *sex* and *age* (*see* Case IX.). The example related, and others only less striking, may well encourage, in similar cases, a persevering trial of sulphur waters. There is nothing in medical science contrary to the view that the gradual alterative effects of sulphur may be competent to confront and reverse a process of rapid disorganization in the joints. Only prolonged observation in a somewhat rare class of cases can establish or disprove it.

The use of the Strathpeffer waters in diseases of the *skin*, and in *sciatica*, and other painful disorders, is described in the section on Baths.

"Great numbers," writes a resident in Strathpeffer, in 1792, "have resorted hither and use the waters of this mineral for all kinds of disorders, without exception."(!) He then goes on to say: "Most benefit has been derived from this mineral, by those troubled with scorbutic complaints, and all kinds of external sores upon the body. It has been used with success in the gravel and stomach complaints."

There is a species of satisfaction to be derived from learning that the indiscriminate use, and abuse, of the waters, however imprudent and likely to disappoint, has, at all events, the respectable sanction of old custom. But there is also in this passage the specification, by an evidently acute observer, of those affections which really did benefit by drinking the sulphur spring. Thus one finds in this century-old enumeration, substituting a more modern phraseology : *scrofulous* affections ; *skin* affections; (chronic) affections of the *stomach* (indigestion and its allies), with calculous affections of the *kidneys* and their district.

These are among the chief disorders most favourably influenced by the same waters to-day. Some others, such as *gout* with its associated disorders, and *rheumatism*, and chronic affections of the *liver*, seem to have been happily unknown in the old time among the class of people then frequenting the springs. But now they are found in large numbers, and to none is the Sulphur Treatment more appropriate. Therefore, with exceptions or additions easily accounted for, the old verdict coincides very nearly with the modern one ; and the fact may perhaps be taken as a testimony to the general truth of both of them.

CHAPTER V

TWO roads are open for bringing sulphur, under the form of sulphur water, into the body. The *internal* use, by the stomach, is by far the more important and more certain ; but if entrance be here denied from temporary causes or excessive delicacy of that organ, another way is open, namely the *external* use of these waters in the form of lotions and baths. It is now admitted by all authorities that sulphuretted hydrogen is absorbed by the skin, and in this respect the Sulphur Bath differs from almost all other known (natural) mineral baths, in which, it is believed, no real absorption takes place. The subtle and penetrating quality of sulphuretted hydrogen gas is here once more illustrated. Under the *internal* use of the water it makes its way, as has been already observed, outwards to the skin ; and under its *external* use in the form of baths there is good evidence that the sulphur finds its way to the internal organs. By whatever way admitted, the action of sulphur is always the same in character. When warm sulphur baths are employed the effect of the *Warm Bath* is of course added to that of the absorbed gas, and thus becomes an important auxiliary to the internal use of the waters, particularly when it is desired to make an impression on parts near the surface, such as the joints and skin.

The second, and secondary, avenue of entrance is therefore by the *skin*, and with reference to this structure, which was purposely omitted from the section on Medicinal Effects, a brief digression must now be made. Among the other tissues and organs affected by the action of sulphur this one holds an important place. The skin is an organ exposed to many and various departures from health, some of them connected in an important manner with constitutional disorders. It may be simply dry, partially obstructed, sluggish, or over-sensitive : or, not only function but nutrition may be at fault, causing what are commonly called "skin affections," such as eczema and psoriasis. It is a matter of experience that some of these conditions of *perverted nutrition* in the skin are remarkably under the control of remedies, of which sulphur is one. In fact the main title of sulphur as a remedy is founded on its *alterative* action, that is to say on its power to influence nutrition. That, then, is the first mode, namely as an alterative or specific, in which sulphur acts upon the skin. It exhibits, however, in addition a *local* action either on the skin or the mucous membrane to which it is applied ; and some esteemed writers have described also a "remote local action" of sulphuretted hydrogen, not manifested at the point of application, but on tissues like the skin and joints, to which it is carried in the course of circulation. This, however would seem to be essentially an alterative action, produced in those parts selected by the remedy. In its true local action sulphur is stimulant to the vascular and sedative to the nervous systems, and hence probably the effect of outward applications in relieving pain.*

To obtain these acknowledged therapeutic effects upon the skin the two avenues already referred to are generally both employed. The main reliance is in all cases placed on the stomach, but the way of the skin possesses, in disorders of that organ, the additional advantage of local action just referred to. The first having been already dealt with in another section, it now remains to describe the use of the second—the road by the skin.

The Strathpeffer Sulphur Baths contain hardly a trace of mineral, that is of saline, constituents. In this important respect they differ from the baths of Harrogate, which, in addition to sulphur, contain a large quantity of chloride of sodium. The latter is the main constituent of sea-water and of brine baths, such as those of Droitwich ; and baths so impregnated have, as a matter of experience, an exciting and irritating effect on the skin unknown to the pure sulphur bath.

In addition to the question of saline matter, some importance attaches to the form in which the sulphur

---

* *Materia Medica and Therapeutics,* by J. Mitchell Bruce, M.A. M.D., p. 136.

itself occurs. Dr. Braun,* whose classical work has
been already quoted, adopts the modern view that
alkaline sulphides cannot be absorbed by the skin.
The specific effect of the sulphur bath must therefore
be referred to free sulphuretted hydrogen. In this
connection it is worthy of notice that some of the most
famous thermal sulphur baths are almost destitute
of this gas! Of those in the Pyrences, for example,
Barèges has none, Luchon and Cauterets only traces.
The sulphur at these Spas is in alkaline combination.
On the other hand, in the Strathpeffer sulphur bath
almost the entire sulphur is present in the gaseous
form—in the form, that is to say, most favourable to
absorption. With a soft water, free of briny salts, and
holding its sulphur—(the wells used for bathing are here
referred to)—in the gaseous form, Strathpeffer affords
every facility for the rational use of sulphur externally.

The storage and heating of the water—two operations
not without difficulty, but upon which the utility of
the baths largely depends—have been greatly improved
at Strathpeffer within the most recent years. In both
these operations sulphur gas is apt to escape ; and, in
recent improvements and some which still remain to
be carried out, the endeavour has been to obtain a
sulphur bath with the *least possible* loss of sulphur.
Having as a starting-point a strongly sulphuretted water,
it should not be difficult, accepting the guidance of

---

* See *Curative Effects of Baths and Waters*, p. 267.

5

experience, to provide at Strathpeffer a sulphur bath
far richer in the gaseous ingredient than any of the
Continental thermal baths.

The sulphur bath is usually taken at about blood heat,
but sometimes at more extreme temperatures, ranging
from 80° to 110°, according to the indications for
thermal treatment. After the bath, it is now usual to
use a "dry pack" of hot linen, by which the bather
lying on a couch is dried without exertion : for fatigue,
particularly after a *hot* bath, is inadvisable. Baths
of this kind should never be taken by persons subject
to faintness or fits ; and, in cases of organic disease,
only with great caution and by direction.

The sulphur bath is useful for dry and sluggish and
irritable skins, and for many varieties of *eczema*. Among
these may be particularly mentioned : chronic dry
eczema, sometimes associated with gout* (*see* Cases I.
and II.) ; and also the distressing form often met with in
middle-aged persons of stout habit, particularly ladies,
of moist relapsing eczema of the body. The soothing
effect of the bath is here very remarkable, but an internal
use of the waters is nearly always recommended as well.
In other cases of irritable, moist localized eczema, a *lotion*
of the water is often found beneficial. The same kind
of bath is employed for *psoriasis* and for *chronic rheumatism* and *gout* (*see* Cases III. to VII.) Among severe and
chronic affections of the skin, experience shows that those

---

* See the Author's "Observations on the Ætiology of Eczema,"
Brit. Med. Journ., 23rd April 1887.

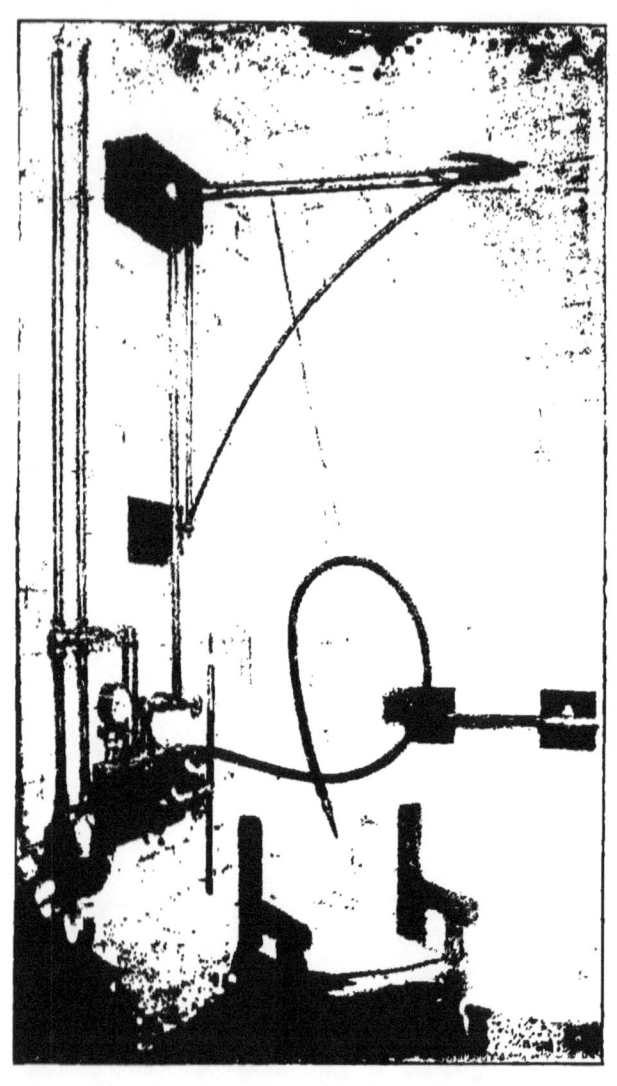

LADIES' DOUCHE-ROOM AND APPARATUS.

are always more amenable to Sulphur Water Treatment which are associated with the gouty constitution.

From the foregoing observations the medical reader may observe that *Thermal Treatment*, as a curative agency, is not disregarded at Strathpeffer. It forms a most important and most rational auxiliary to a Sulphur Spa, for, to many cases, Thermal Treatment as an external, and Sulphur as an internal, remedy are in combination admirably adapted. And it is only when patients are enabled, as at Spas, to adjust their lives for some weeks to rather exacting requirements, that it is possible to attempt the one or the other.

One of the most important forms of Thermal Treatment is by the *Douche*. This has now been introduced for some years at Strathpeffer, and excellent results are obtained from its use, both in the ordinary form and in a special form of spinal douche. The Ladies' Douche Room, with apparatus newly fitted up after a special design, is here represented. In addition to rheumatic and gouty conditions of the joints, the nozzle douche is employed in painful affections of the nerves and muscles, —for example, sciatica and muscular rheumatism (*see* Cases VIII. and XII.). Electrical Treatment and Massage may or may not be combined with this treatment.

The *Spinal Douche* as employed at Strathpeffer is, in the author's belief, a somewhat new form of Thermal Treatment. This douche consists of very fine horizontal jets in a vertical series, and is received upon the spine from a perforated metal stand at a few inches distance. The water is generally used at a considerable pressure and temperature, the latter from 112° to 120° or even 130.° The patient being comfortably seated the while, the application is continued for ten, fifteen, or twenty minutes; and the temperature and pressure of the douche varied or alternated at will by the attendant, without altering the position of the apparatus. This treatment is particularly valued for its vaso-motor effects. Among the affections that have hitherto benefited from its use may be named *dysmenorrhœa, nervous prostration* (neurasthenia), and also conditions of *defective circulation* and *sluggish action* of the abdominal organs. Some curious instances of laxative effect have been noticed, and it is a common observation that the douche "brings a glow of heat" into the extremities.

The After-bath Treatment is a matter of some importance with this form of Thermal Treatment. It is to be regretted that so far no arrangements have been provided for conveying persons direct from the bath-rooms to their beds, as at Aix-les-Bains—the home *par excellence* of Thermal Treatment. A system of "porteurs" and sedans, such as have lately been introduced at Bath, would greatly facilitate this important treatment at Strathpeffer.

A notable addition is about to be made to the Bathing Establishment at Strathpeffer in the shape of a well-appointed *Peat,* or *Moor, Bath.* The want of this bath at the Home Spas has long been felt; and indeed, no small discredit has attached to them for obliging medical men to send their patients to Germany for a bath that should long ago have been forthcoming in this country. To no place is the Peat Bath more appropriate than Strathpeffer, where Nature has richly supplied the requisite materials. The disintegrated peat, which exists in enormous deposits on the shoulders of Ben Wyvis, will be conveyed to the Spa and reduced to a coarse powder. It may be used either as a plain peat bath or in combination with sulphur water. Much advantage is anticipated from the introduction, probably for the first time in this country, of so valuable and important a mode of treatment. It is employed as a thermal agency in obstinate skin affections, and more especially for its effect in promoting the absorption of exudations in affections of the joints.

The *Pine Bath*, prepared from the well-known extract, may be also obtained at Strathpeffer, if desired. It is used by an increasing number of visitors on account of its agreeable aromatic quality.

In association with Thermal Treatment, and for independent employment, much importance is now rightly attached to *Massage.* This invaluable treatment is particularly appropriate to a spa ; for the reason already referred to, that in spa life is the grand opportunity for the more precise, prolonged, and exacting modes of cure. A thoroughly competent *Masseur* from London is in attendance at Strathpeffer during the season, and there is also an excellent *Masseuse.**

* Mrs. Ross, Cromarty Buildings.

CHAPTER VI.

THE Chalybeate, or Iron, Spring lately conveyed to the Pump Room, rises near the Raven Rock, three miles distant, where it has been known, probably for centuries, as the "Saints' Well." It is one of a group occurring in the neighbourhood, all more or less similar in character, but which have hitherto attracted but little attention. The pedestrian will notice here and there springs with a bright ochre-coloured deposit (carbonated oxide of iron). One of the most remarkable of these, which has a strong chalybeate flavour, is found on the railway a little west of Auchterneed station.

In all these springs the iron exists as a carbonate, which would be quite insoluble did not the water contain an excess of free carbonic acid gas. Therefore, it follows that exposure to the air, by dissipating this gas, allows the iron to fall as a precipitate. In the Saints' Well Chalybeate, when quite fresh, gas is often present in great abundance, far more abundantly than would appear from the analysis, which was made in

Edinburgh on water bottled from the open well.* In fact it sometimes comes with an almost explosive force at the Pump Room fountain, and, when allowed to run slowly, has an opalescence like that of champagne. As the effervescence proceeds, the water gradually clears. On allowing it to stand aside for two or three days, a brown sediment of the oxide of iron falls to the bottom of the glass, and the surface exposed to the air is coated with the same oxide as a thin iridescent pellicle.

ANALYSIS OF THE CHALYBEATE WATER OF STRATHPEFFER.
BY DR. STEVENSON MACADAM.

ANALYTICAL LABORATORY, SURGEONS' HALL,
EDINBURGH, July 6th, 1871.

Analysis of sample of water from Saints' Well, Strathpeffer.

One Imperial Gallon contains :—

	Grains.
Carbonate of Iron . . .	2·46
Carbonate of Lime .	3·14
Chloride of Sodium . .	1·17
Sulphate of Lime . .	1·13
Chloride of Magnesium . . .	0·38
Carbonate of Magnesia . .	0·41
Phosphates . . .	0·19
Soluble Silica . .	0·21
Organic Matter .	0·47

Total Matter dissolved in Imperial Gallon 9·56
    Hardness 7½°

* At the time of Dr. Macadam's analysis the spring was exposed

Cubic Inches.

Total Gases dissolved in Imperial Gallon   12·68

Percentage Composition of the Gases—

Cubic Inches.

Carbonic Acid	31·98
Oxygen	20·34
Nitrogen	47·68
	———
	100·00

What has been already said in a previous chapter regarding the medicinal effects of mineral waters applies with especial force to the class of which the Strathpeffer Chalybeate is one.   It is well known that the absorbing power of the stomach for iron is extremely limited; and that the most effective absorption is in general obtained when very *small doses* are presented in *dilute solution.*   The amount of iron required by the blood is itself minute; and could readily be made up, if absorption were active, by a natural Chalybeate like that of Strathpeffer, with a quarter of a grain of the carbonate dissolved in sixteen ounces.

The first effect of this chalybeate is stimulating, occasionally in a marked degree, giving rise to feelings of exhilaration, flushing of the head and even staggering.

---

to the air.   When it was at a later date carefully closed in at the source, the gaseous contents appeared to be much increased.   No further analysis has been made; and whether the free gas now present in the water at the Pump Room is all carbonic acid gas has not been sufficiently determined.   It is curiously variable in amount and is sometimes nearly absent.

Ladies, in particular, have sometimes complained that the "iron water intoxicated" them. The same observation has often been made in the use of similar waters at Spa, Pyrmont, and other places. These effects are due to the presence of Carbonic Acid Gas. This gas imparts to the water not only a pleasant and refreshing taste, but also a light and digestible quality, adapted to delicate stomachs. Hence the Chalybeate can often be borne, and is in fact repeatedly taken with advantage, where ordinary Iron Treatment is quite inadmissible,—for example, in the common case where poverty of blood in young persons is complicated by indigestion and irritability of the stomach. The water, drunk in effervescence, stimulates the appetite and the digestive process in virtue of the carbonic acid gas, whilst the tonic effects due to the absorption of iron afterwards follow.

In addition to common *anæmia* and *indigestion* of younger life, the Chalybeate exerts a valuable influence at a later age in persons of relaxed and debilitated habit, more particularly in those affected by a commencing degenerative disease of the blood-vessels and kidneys (*Cf.* Cases IV., V., and XV.). The same is true of debility and anæmia of malarious origin (*see* Case XIV). Finally, a short course of this water is not infrequently prescribed as a tonic, after a longer period of Sulphur Treatment. On the other hand, those who come to drink the iron spring are in some cases benefited by a week or two of sulphur, to pave the way for the tonic water.

A recent improvement in the service of this water is worthy of notice, a heating apparatus of approved construction having been adapted to it. Warmth, as in the case of the sulphur water, favours absorption, and so materially intensifies the Chalybeate action.*

* See the Author's " Observations on the Use of the Effervescing Chalybeate of Strathpeffer Spa," *Brit. Med. Journ.,* May 5th, 1888.

CHAPTER VII.

THE object of this section is to exemplify by the narrative of actual cases the treatment pursued, and precautions observed, at Strathpeffer Spa. No impersonal description can quite so well illustrate *for the invalid* the many important practical points arising in the course of each case ; or can, *for the general reader*, furnish so true an estimate of what may be called the *sanative capacity* of the place.

CASE I.—An active gentleman, aged 72, of spare habit, had been the subject of *chronic eczema* from the age of 47, although he had been temporarily cured more than once under different kinds of treatment. The autumn before visiting Strathpeffer the eczema "came out" very severely, the whole body being covered, excepting the face, hands and feet. In the summer he came to the Wells "scaling and powdering." At this time the irritation of the skin was so excessive as to preclude sleep. He was at once put upon the sulphur water and baths, and of the latter took twenty-three in four weeks. The treatment during this time had no appreciable effect, excepting to improve the digestion, and cure some old and troublesome hæmorrhoids. On returning to his home from Strathpeffer, the eczema "diminished by slow and imperceptible degrees," and had entirely disappeared in eight months. The following summer this gentleman came back, for a short "preventive course," in excellent health, no further eczema having appeared. At the present time, five years later, he remains free from eczema.

The above-noted *late effects* of a course of mineral water are not infrequent, even in the most successful cases. The subjects of skin affections, in particular, often find it necessary to persevere with patience, until the cure, if one may say so, has had time to come to the surface. Happily, in these cases, when improvement does come, it nearly always is, " though late-reaped, yet long-enduring." The process of healing is here *from within outwards*, the disorder being not suppressed, but rather-expelled ; and hence external sores, which many have regarded as safety-valves to the sick man, are daily cured by Mineral Waters and other constitutional remedies without the slightest risk to health.

CASE II.—A lady, aged 45, of a gouty family, complains of *eczema* of the hands, of one year's duration—at first moist, afterwards dry. The eczema did well for the first fortnight at the Spa ; but much resented an ill-advised indulgence in salmon, becoming thereafter hot, moist, and inflamed as at the first. However, after another three weeks of the treatment, with greater care in diet, the skin affection is reported "quite gone," and the general health much improved.

CASE III.—A gentleman, aged 54, of a strongly *gouty* family, who has been much abroad, but has always been a careful liver, paid his first visit to Strathpeffer shortly after sustaining an attack of his old enemy in the foot. The waters agreed perfectly—moderate doses only being required, with a few baths ; and, after a fortnight, he was "much improved ; walking three miles." The next season, no attack of gout having occurred in the interval, he returned for a second course of water. On this occasion, the baths "brought out" at first pains in the limbs—especially in a sprained joint—the pains lasting two or three days. This proved as usual, a favourable symptom, and the patient again left much improved. In the third year, three weeks of the same treatment were taken. This time another attack had just occurred in the foot, and the first baths again "brought out" the pains rather severely ; but with admirable perseverance, he went through the usual course, and left once more much better. Two years later this gentleman returned again, saying that he had had some "twinges" of gout, but otherwise his health was good. A short course was a fourth time prescribed rather by way of prevention than cure.

CASE IV.—This was the case of a gentleman, aged 57,

who had suffered from several attacks of *gout*, as well as from " sciatica " and "lumbago." The first year he improved under the Sulphur Water Treatment, and baths were taken on alternate days. The following season,—1886, he returned, having suffered some slight attacks of gout in the interval. The presence of other symptoms now made the sulphur inadmissible, and the effervescing Chalybeate was given with good effect as a tonic—three glasses daily. Although in an earlier stage Iron Treatment would not be in general applicable to the gouty patient, yet in cases such as these, which are not infrequent at Strathpeffer, the Chalybeate is a really useful remedy—in the treatment not of gout, but of the more serious affections arising out of it.

This gentleman returned in 1887 and reported that he had had since the previous year " repeated attacks " of normal gout, for which he had visited Bath. This change in his case was very satisfactory, for it was accompanied by an improvement in the more serious (organic) symptoms. He again went through his course : sulphur water for ten days, iron for three weeks ; and went away looking and feeling better, with good appetite and able to walk several miles. At a fourth visit (1888) he again took a short course of the same treatment ; which, taken thus annually, seems to have an excellent effect in aiding the *development* and *removal* of gouty matter.

CASE V.—A successful man of business, aged 63,

who has seen much hard work as a decorator and painter, falls into serious ill-health a little more than two years before coming to the Spa. He has suffered from severe attacks of gout for twenty-five years, and benefited much from visits to Harrogate. Since the recent illness of two years ago, he has been in a state of more or less weakness and prostration, with "indigestion," weak and irregular action of the heart, and chronic soreness and swelling of the feet. Six months ago he was again ill, and this time the heart's action was seriously affected, and the digestive organs and kidneys much deranged. On arrival at the Spa it was evident that in this case, as in the one last described, organic changes were present, together with and overshadowing the directly gouty symptoms.

In these circumstances Mineral Water, and particularly Mineral Bath, Treatment if attempted must be used with the greatest caution, and ample time allowed. After a week, a beginning was made with half a pint of the strongest sulphur water at noon. He was encouraged to walk a few steps in the open air, and in particular to limit alcoholic stimulants in the strictest way. In another fortnight a pint and a half of the strong well was being daily taken, and Douche Baths applied to the feet with systematic Medical Rubbing. A month after arrival he was able to walk half a mile on the stretch, and had ventured on two sulphur baths. The sulphur waters were continued in all for five weeks; and then, after an interval, a fortnight's course of the Chalybeate

6

taken. Douches and Massage were kept up throughout. Daily drives and short walks were also observed as part of the treatment. In two months he left, greatly better in all respects.

CASE VI.—A married lady, aged 32, had for the last four years often suffered from " rheumatism " and " rheumatic gout." She comes of a family in which both gout and rheumatism are prevalent, and has evidently inherited a strong predisposition to these affections. This is nearly certain to manifest itself from time to time in the course of her life, and should be combated by appropriate treatment, undertaken at regular intervals, until the tendency has subsided. Warning symptoms will sometimes, in a case of this kind, be overlooked by the patient and even by the medical adviser, but to no class of cases is the treatment by Mineral Waters and Baths better adapted. This lady entered with spirit into a brief course of two or three weeks, during two successive seasons. The Baths " brought out " the pains rather sharply, but neither sleep nor appetite suffered, and she left the Spa better in every respect.

CASE VII. —This case, also a lady, presents in many points a contrast to the last. Being 78 years of age, she had suffered from " rheumatism " (rather acutely) for about one year, the larger joints being alone affected, with stiffness, some pain and crackling. Great improvement followed the use of a few Sulphur Baths.

[It may be noted *en passant* that the Sulphur Bath may be safely given to elderly and invalid persons without fear of injurious consequences, if due precautions are observed—as, of course, in *every* case is more or less requisite.]

CASE VIII.—This may be said to resemble Case VI., inasmuch as the patient owed her complaint mainly to constitutional causes. The lady had been much abroad, in hot climates, and her family history gave evidence both to gout and rheumatism. The painful affection was, with her, confined to one joint, where it had settled persistently for seven or eight years. It was, however, completely overcome by a persevering course of Douche Baths, combined with an internal use of the water in small doses.

CASE IX.—A mother of a family, aged 42, is suddenly affected for the first time with what is described as "acute rheumatism in all the joints." She keeps her bed for three months; and then, shortly after rising, a relapse comes on, confining her again to bed; from which she is unable to rise for six months. She is carried to Strathpeffer, unable to stand or walk. Many of the small joints of the hand are stiff. The knees and some other large joints are swollen, painful, and useless. Very little was attempted at the Spa beyond carefully regulated drinking of the sulphur waters, but of these she came to take a large daily allowance.

A little Medical Rubbing was cautiously administered ; and as soon as possible the patient was assisted into the open air. Her achievements in the way of locomotion were truly wonderful. The first was to stand at the table ; the second to take a step or two behind a chair. Eventually she circumnavigated the table by leaning heavily upon it, and at length she was able to walk a short distance with a crutch. Indeed, on one occasion before leaving Strathpeffer, she covered in this way half a mile. It must be added that this case is in every way an exceptional one. The happy result was doubtless aided by her strong faith in the remedy to which she had come, and the persevering use of it for a period of *three months.* Medically considered, the case appears to belong. to a small group, better understood now than formerly, and in which treatment very often fails of its effect. Even a solitary record of benefit may encourage the practitioner to try the use of sulphur waters for this distressing malady.

CASE X. is that of a gentleman of stout habit, in later middle life, who had seen much service in tropical countries. He complained of "indigestion" and "lumbago," and was found to have some enlargement of the liver and a weak action of the heart ; but benefited greatly by three weeks of the water.

This case is typical of an important and definite group. Men, sometimes of great constitutional energy and natives of temperate regions, have been subjected

year after year to the slowly debilitating effects of a
tropical *climate*; to which probably they did not adapt
themselves by the appropriate change in diet and mode
of life. They have also, perhaps, at one time or another,
been exposed, in especially unhealthy districts, to the
insidious approaches of *disease*. Yet an apparent im-
munity from these ills has been long enjoyed—thanks
to an originally sound constitution, and the avoidance
of more flagrant dangers; and the damage, unconsciously
sustained, is only discovered in later life. Such are
frequent at all the Spas and Baths, and this fact alone
bears strong testimony to the efficacy, in these cases
also, of Mineral Water Treatment.

[Somewhat akin to the case last quoted are those in
which, in this country, the liver is chiefly at fault.
They go under the names: "Torpid," or "Sluggish,"
Liver, "Biliousness," "Biliary Colic," *etc.* In most or
all such the circulation of this organ is deranged; and
waters—especially thermal, or hot, waters—are effica-
cious, by reason of the powerful "flushing" they ad-
minister to the circulatory system of the liver. When to
this rousing influence upon the circulation is added the
peculiarly stimulating effect of the sulphur elements,
we indicate the two essential features of the Strathpeffer
treatment in such cases.]

CASE XI.—A young lady, aged 17, always a little
delicate, has suffered slightly from malarial influence

in the Mediterranean.   In her case this seems to take
the form of digestive derangements.   Four months later,
having returned home, there follows an attack of acute
catarrhal jaundice, with high febrile reaction and great
prostration.   A fortnight afterwards, having been brought
to Strathpeffer, she commences, with great caution, a
mild course of sulphur water.   In spite of the digestive
delicacy, this is exceedingly well borne; with the result
that after three weeks the jaundice has entirely disappeared, and a healthy strength and colour returned.

It would be impossible to conceive a case more suited
than this to sulphur waters.

CASE XII.—A gentleman, of nearly 35 years, had
suffered once from gout, two years ago; since then,
from flying muscular pains.   After travelling to the Spa
from Ireland, he was seized with a smart attack of
sciatica.   This, with the " rheumatism," quickly yielded
to the hot Douche, frequently repeated, sulphur water
being taken in the meantime for the general condition.

The Douche, administered in this manner, at high
temperatures and pressures, is very often a perfect
remedy in painful muscular affections of this kind; but
it must be used with precaution, precision, and perseverance.

CASE XIII.—Another example of *sciatica*, successfully
treated in a somewhat different manner, may be here
recorded.   A gentleman, aged 60, had suffered from

a severe reducing illness twenty-five years since, and with rheumatic stiffness and pain occasionally for fifteen years. Four months before arriving at the Spa sciatica came on after riding on the outside of a street car. Stiffness of the muscles was a prominent symptom. He was recommended Sulphur Water from the Upper Well, and systematic Massage, with occasional Baths. To the Massage the lion's share of the credit rightly belongs, but in Spa life and regimen it found its opportunity. Within three weeks of arrival this gentleman had made the ascent of Ben Wyvis on foot, which is always to be regarded in such cases as an undoubted proof of cure.

CASE XIV.—A lady, aged about 45, after much mental strain and bodily illness (dysentery and "fevers") in tropical South America, returned home in ailing health, subject to recurring "internal chills," diarrhœa, and general weakness. She was stout, very anæmic, nervous, with frequent indigestion, headaches and flying pains. . For nearly four weeks this lady took the Chalybeate, usually hot, and latterly to the extent of forty-five ounces daily. With this were combined occasional Douches, Sulphur Baths, and Massage; which no doubt contributed to a striking improvement in nervous, muscular, and digestive tone. For cases of this kind a very prolonged, and perhaps intermittent, use of the water is to be recommended, repeated from year to year where benefit has been once derived.

Case XV. The last case to be cited is another example of Chalybeate Treatment. A gentleman, aged 71, had lost health for a year, with some swelling of the extremities, and increasing pallor of the skin, although no serious failure in any organ could be detected. The effervescing tonic water was taken regularly for some weeks, and produced a most happy improvement, both in the appearance and in the strength. Of course, as in other cases, the repose of Spa life, and the invigorating air, deserve some of the credit. This we need not grudge them, whilst, at the same time, fully persuaded of the restorative character of all the means used.

CHAPTER VIII.

SPA LIFE AND DIET—THE "SEASON."

STRATHPEFFER AS A WINTER RESORT.

MONG the restorative conditions of life at a Spa are embraced these four :—Climate and Waters ; Change in Manner of Life and in Diet. Health-seekers can hardly escape the first of these, or overlook the second ; but the third and fourth are perhaps equally important, and these, unfortunately, it is very common to neglect. The Climate and Waters of Strathpeffer having been already discussed, it remains to indicate very briefly some of the more essential points in Life and Diet which the visitor may properly observe.

Let him then in the first place accept the principle of **Change**—it may be greater or less, in his habits and manner of living. Without it he cannot obtain the full measure of benefit. Outside this general necessity of change, there are the greatest possible differences of degree. Some are sunk so deep in unhealthy grooves that they need a complete mental and physical revolution. In others it is sufficient to occupy the *Mind* alone with

something new. For this latter class, which is a large
one, the Health Resorts of this country have unfortunately
as yet made but indifferent provision. Many seeking
renewal of health come from a life of mental labour and
strain, and bring their overwrought brains with them.
Such as these cannot " sit on a cliff and look at the
sea ! " The agency which alone can " unbend the bow "
must *possess* it and be exerted within it. Let such a one,
if possible, bring friends with him ; or if not, condescend
to make them. Let him enjoy good music, pleasant
company, light literature; or better still, discover an
interest in investigating the antiquities or natural
curiosities of the district ; or, if strong enough, find
pleasurable excitement in a little mountaineering. As
a warning and a caution, let all remember the old and
true saying—

" *There is no cure for those who care.*"

There is one particular in which change must be as
thorough as possible. No man can rid himself of disorder without first ridding his life of the cause of his
disorder. This applies in particular to meats and drinks,
from which all ascertained causes of the present trouble
must be rigidly excluded. Many who seek benefit
obtain none from failing to conform to this rule.

Since only chronic affections are admissible to mineral
water treatment, the course of improvement, even in the
most favourable circumstances, is usually gradual. *Perseverance* is therefore requisite, in correcting, it may be,

some slowly-acquired constitutional defect, like gout; or some defective state of absorption or nutrition, like dyspepsia or eczema. Experience shows that such disorders do yield in a remarkable manner to sulphur water and baths, but it may be well, in a prolonged course, to intermit treatment for a while. Where decided benefit has been derived from a mineral water, it is matter of common prudence to repeat year by year, as often as it may be needful, a form of treatment which is, perhaps more than any other truly eradicative.

Visitors at the Spa are enjoined not only to retire, but to *rise, early*. The first glass of sulphur water should be taken at least an hour and a half before breakfast; and it is far better if possible to take it at the Wells. The cool, fresh, early hours of the summer's day or the crisp clear morning in October are to be enjoyed out of doors, with as much walking exercise as may be suitable to the case. This, as has been wittily remarked, greatly assists the digestion of the water, on the principle *solvitur ambulando.* After breakfast and a short rest, the invalid is encouraged, when the day is fine, to try another spell of *moderate exercise.* Measured walks have not yet been marked out, but any one may note for himself the increase of his excursion day by day—for example, on the hillside of Kinettas. Even delicate and debilitated persons, and those suffering from organic weakness—for example, of the heart—are strongly advised to get daily upon the higher levels, north and south of the valley. For those who are a little more robust,

there is the Golf Course and the quiet amusement of
bowls, both valuable from the gentle continuous bodily
exercise they provide. But besides these, there are
many who benefit by more vigorous exertion. Those
accustomed to a sedentary or luxurious life will often
find that a long hill-climb daily, horse exercise, and lawn
tennis greatly enhance the benefit of Mineral Water and
Dietetic Treatment.

It is impossible to state any scheme of **Diet** applicable
to all cases; for, indeed, the regimen in this respect is
very often a matter for most careful individual study.
A few hints of a general character may, however,
prove useful. *Be temperate*, is the first law of health.
Those who sit down to a prolonged *table d'hôte* may
prudently remember the saying of Hesiod, "He is a
fool who does not understand how much the half is
better than the whole." Never eat unless hungry;
drink little or nothing with meals during the course of
waters; take all meals in company, and eat slowly;
avoid all alcoholic stimulants. Whatever may be true
in ordinary life, the great majority of cases do far better
at spas without alcohol. The few who persist, against
advice, in habits of artificial stimulation, even in the
free and healthful atmosphere of spa life, generally
discover to their cost that the alcohol has defeated any
benefit they might have gained. On the other hand,
there are conditions of ill-health, both at spas and elsewhere, in which alcoholic remedies are very properly
prescribed.

The following outline of diet is very often observed at Strathpeffer with advantage : For breakfast, at *half-past eight* or nine, coffee, with toast and eggs, or chop, avoiding fat; a nominal lunch, perhaps a little cold chicken and bread, at one; dinner at six or seven (no soup or entrées), fish or game, good beef, or mutton, or venison, tender green vegetables but no cabbage, sparingly of potatoes, little or no farinaceous dishes, no pastry, plenty of cooked fruit; after dinner, a small cup of coffee; if hungry, a biscuit and glass of water at bedtime. In regard to fresh fruit, no objection is taken, unless in particular cases, to strawberries and grapes. Finally, if any general character can be assigned to a diet in harmony with the use of the Strathpeffer waters, it should be good in quality, in quantity moderate, well-cooked, plain, varied, and dry.

It is generally stated that the "**Season**" at Strathpeffer Spa extends from May to October, both months included. The climatic characters of the several months are exhibited in the diagram at page 17. It is to be observed that from April to August there is a period of small rainfall, the entire summer being drier at the Spa than in London. In the months May and June, Sulphur Treatment is taken with great advantage; and sometimes a short course of a fortnight or three weeks in these months is supplemented, in suitable cases, by a second visit later in the year.

Those who desire to avoid the crowd of the season,

and at the same time to obtain the waters in their prime autumnal condition, have been accustomed to visit the Spa in October. This is now becoming more and more usual, and the practice has much to recommend it. October is usually a fine month at Strathpeffer. There are in most years a few night frosts towards the end of the month, but the mean temperature is only a little below that of May. Among recent years, the October of 1888 was slightly warmer at Strathpeffer than at Greenwich. To the lover of clear skies, exquisite autumnal tints, and sunsets, this month in Scotland has great charms.

A minute description of the **Winter Climate** based upon observations extending over five winters, has been given in an earlier chapter. The warmth of the nights and the bright sunshine of the days, with the great freedom from mist and fog, are perhaps its most striking features.

It is important to remember that the character of greatest value in a winter health resort is not high temperature, but pure, dry air, bright sunshine, and perhaps the neighbourhood of mountains. If these be provided, it is well known that persons of great delicacy, and affected by serious pulmonary disease, rather benefit than otherwise by a certain amount of exposure to cold. At Davos Platz the night (minimum) temperatures for the winter months are *very far below* those of Strathpeffer; whilst, owing to the effects of bright sunshine, the day (maximum) temperatures arc only slightly colder than the same readings at the Scottish resort. The difference between night and day,—daily range—is, therefore, much greater at Davos than at Strathpeffer. The latter, indeed, as may be seen from the diagram, has a remarkably *small daily range* for a sunny winter station.

The more fully the several features of the climate arc examined, the more clearly is Strathpeffer seen to possess the cardinal qualifications for a **Bracing Winter Health Resort.** There are numerous cases of pulmonary disease, some incipient, others recurrent or advancing— in which Climate is certainly the most hopeful, and perhaps the only curative, treatment. Many of these arc able to take a certain amount of exercise, on foot or horseback, and arc always the better for it. Where should such spend the winter ? Rather than a moist relaxing climate, do they not need one more directly bracing, with dry sunny mountain air ? If at the same time they are comfortably housed,* encouraged to clothe warmly, live well, and avoid the occasional east winds of spring, experience has already shown in a striking manner that cases of this kind spend the winter at Strathpeffer with great benefit. For those who approve Dr. Bergeon's treatment of Phthisis, it may be added that the sulphur springs contain at this season (*see* p. 44) their strong " winter charge " of sulphuretted hydrogen.

---

* Particular care is needed to select those houses that are best fitted for winter accommodation.

PART II.

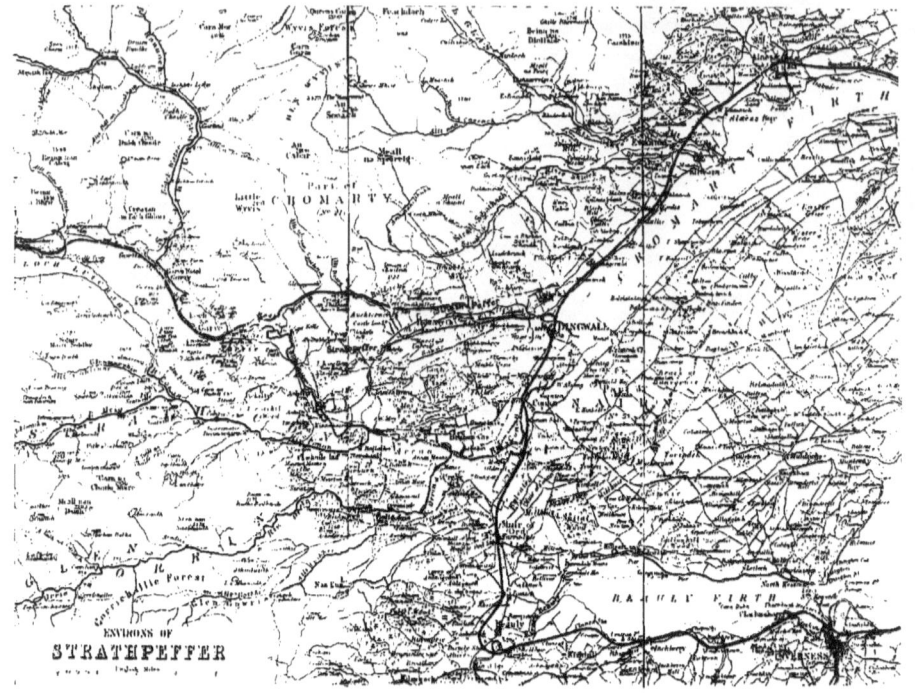

ENVIRONS OF
STRATHPEFFER

CHAPTER IX.

He looks abroad into the varied field
Of Nature, and, though poor perhaps compared
With those whose mansions glitter in his sight,
Calls the delightful scenery all his own.
His are the mountains, and the valleys his,
And the resplendent rivers. . . .

    Nor rural sights alone, but rural sounds
Exhilarate the spirit and restore
The tone of languid Nature.

                     COWPER.

E have already seen what important aids are walking exercise and abundance of open air in the course of Spa Treatment. Happily, visitors to Strathpeffer have a wide choice of shorter and longer foot excursions and drives, suited to all capacities and stages of recovery. On the northern side of the valley there is a pathway ascending right and left above the old burial-ground. Taking the right-hand path and skirting the plantation, a pedestrian of even very limited powers easily reaches the breezy **Golf Course**, where he will be rewarded by a grand panoramic view. The left-hand path conducts to the summit of

Kinettas Hill, where footpaths have been cut among the trees, and rustic seats and a flagstaff erected.   From this point Lochs Kinellan and Achilty, with a range of western hills, are seen.   On the southern side of the valley, which the visitor is recommended to take by preference in the afternoons, there is the high ground behind the Ben Wyvis Hotel, affording a prospect of the mountain of that name, as well as a capital bird's-eye view of the village of Strathpeffer.   If inclined for a further climb one can go on to the Cat's Back, or Knock Farril; or, keeping the same level, the walk may be extended above the cottages of Park as far as the **Blackmuir Wood.**   At all these points the air is usually more exhilarating than in the valley beneath.

Castle Leod, at one time a residence of the Earls of Cromartie, is situated in a spacious park in close proximity to the Spa on the Dingwall road.   The ivy-covered walls and round turrets of this old baronial pile, built by Sir Rorie McKenzie,* are a prominent feature

* "While yet a young man, Sir Rorie obtained from his father the lands of Culteleod, in the parish of Fodderty. After obtaining these lands Sir Rorie had the territorial designation of Culteleod, and the castle, which he subsequently erected there, in the year 1616, was one of his favourite residences. Culteleod includes within its bounds the lofty Ben Wyvis, the highest mountain in Ross, with its fabulous tenure of rendering to the crown a snowball at Midsummer; as well as the beautiful valley of Strathpeffer, now crowded in the summer and autumn months with visitors, for its Spa and its salubrity."—WILLIAM FRASER, *The Earls of Cromartie* (1876).

in our bird's-eye view of the valley just noted. There
are some fine trees in the park, in particular some
Wellingtonias, and a Spanish chestnut, said to be the
largest in Great Britain, with a girth of twenty-six feet
at the base, and nineteen feet breast high. Castle Leod
is at present held by Frederick Shoolbred, Esq., who
kindly allows visitors at the Spa the privilege of walking
in the park before 9 a.m., as far as the iron fence south
of the Castle.

Beyond Castle Leod lies the little village of **Auchterneed**, portions of which, with the crofts upon the
heights above, were allotted to the veteran soldiers
raised upon the estate who had returned from the
great American War.

Above Auchterneed the Dingwall and Skye Railway
mounts the hill westward, by a steep gradient. A mile
and a half west of Auchterneed Station the line passes
under the shadow of the **Raven Rock** (Creagen Fiothatch,
" Rock of the Raven " or " Echoing Rock "). This precipitous cliff or rock runs almost vertical to a height of
250 feet. It was no doubt thrown into its present form
by a fault in the geological formation, and extraordinary
contortions of the strata can be readily traced on its
northern face. Near at hand rises the Saints' Well or
Strathpeffer Chalybeate Spring. A fine echo may be
obtained off the rock from the hill above the railway.

The pedestrian in quest of fine view and bracing air,
may vary his direction above Auchterneed Station. He
may either cross the burn and follow the footpath on to

the shoulders of Ben Wyvis, where he will probably come across the old Cupped Stone (*vide* Antiquities) and see traces of the Strathpeffer Water supply and Peat Fields; or, keeping to the right above the railway, follow the course of the country road along the "**Heights.**" If he has a relish for Folk Lore—quaint records of an unremembered past—here is a good field for his investigations. Farther on, at the March of Tulloch, are the "standing stones" of which mention is made in the chapter on Antiquities. This entire hillside basks in sunshine, even in the colder months, when the valley is too often in shade. This advantage it enjoys from the circumstance that it is high enough to overlook the ridge of Knock Farril on the south. As, moreover, the ground is sheltered by higher slopes and some plantation on the north, it is admirably suited for winter quarters. It is, therefore, to be hoped that accommodation will be provided near the Railway Station on the lower heights, where winter visitants may avail themselves of the bright sunshine, pure dry air, and proximity of the tonic Chalybeate spings.

Knock Farril, being of particular interest, is separately treated.

The Cat's Back (Druim Chat) is a narrow ridge bounding the valley of Strathpeffer on the south, and runs from the last named hill south-westward to the bluff summit Cnoc Moir. This summit is easiest of ascent if one first gains the ridge at the neck of Knock Farril. The walk along the crest between this point and Cnoc Moir affords a magnificent view—not only of the Strathpeffer valley, the picturesque "heights" above Auchterneed, covered with their patchwork of crofts and crowned by the lofty mass of Ben Wyvis; but also on the south, Loch Ussie, where Kenneth Ohr cast away his prophetic stone before he died, the policies of Brahan, the wide valley of the Conan, and the Beauly Firth and hills of Inverness-shire beyond.

Perhaps the finest view point of any in the district (unless that from the "View Rock" can compete with it) is obtained from Cnoc Moir. It embraces a wide sweep of country to the west, range beyond range of hills carrying the eye across that mountainous tract of Ross-shire which intervenes between Strathpeffer and the west coast. These are the summits that do the climate of the Spa such notable service by combing out the excess of water from the rain-laden air currents, that pass over them from the Atlantic. If a level plain lay between Cnoc Moir and the west coast, the rainfall of Strathpeffer would be double or treble its present quantity. From Cnoc Moir on a clear day one may see seven or eight lochs and rivers,—Loch Ussie and the Beauly Firth to the east; Lochs Kinellan, Achilty, and Garve with smaller unnamed tarns westward among the nearer hills; and southward of these the rivers Blackwater and Conan, enclosing the base of the sugar-loaf-shaped Tor Achilty, and meeting in confluence in the valley below. To vary the route one may return by a path on the southern side of the hill, winding round the precipitous western extremity, and so by way of the Blackmuir Wood to the Spa. This ascent is not a difficult climb, and may be made with great pleasure either in a forenoon, at sunset when the effects are sometimes very lovely, or on a bright moonlight night.

Kinellan Loch and the **View Rock.**—A very pretty walk to Kinellan may be had by taking the footpath through the Kinettas Woods, or one may take the road past the Spa Hotel at the head of the valley. It is unfortunate there is no better carriage access to this charming piece of water, which might also be readily utilized for boating and fishing. Passing along the southern side of the loch, one notices the small island where once was a place of strength of the Seaforths— a rude house founded on oaken logs—now the haunt of water-fowl and an occasional heron. Beyond Kinellan on the north is the cairn-topped hill Craig Ulladaile, where certain small tarns, jewelled with white water-lilies, nestle in the hollows, and the marshes yield the round-leaved and the rarer long-leaved sundews and butterworts without number.

Mounting the hill at the further, or west, end of the Loch, one may either strike off across the moor to Rogie Falls, or, crossing the fence and taking the footpath on the left, make one's way through a short belt of plantation to the View Rock. This is only two miles from the Spa, and is usually taken by visitors in an early stage of their progress. The view is certainly

a fine one, embracing line beyond line of summits—from
Ben Wyvis in the north, to the hills of Fairburn in the
south. In the foreground are Loch Achilty and Tor
Achilty, with Coul House (Sir Arthur Mackenzie, Bart.)
to the left, and the little village of Contin and the
Blackwater below. The geological features of this
prospect are referred to in a later chapter.

From the View Rock, if inclined, one may either take
a stretch northward across the hills to the Skye Railway and Raven's Rock, or strike the Blackwater, which
is due west, and follow it up to the Falls of Rogie, the
latter a charming walk : or finally, one may come down
upon Contin, or cross the river at the Achilty Bridge,
and ascend Tor Achilty. In the last case the pedestrian
must not fail to notice the fine raised beach just above
the Achilty Bridge. The conical or sugar-loaf shape of
Tor Achilty is a prominent feature in many a prospect
of this region. On the Achilty side the slope is gradual
and covered with woods, in which the botanist will find
a favoured haunt. From the summit, with its precipitous
eastern face of conglomerate rock, the eye overlooks
like a map the fertile valley of the Conan.

DRIVES.

The Falls of Rogie, on the Blackwater.—These may
be reached either by a five-miles drive' through pretty
scenery, or a walk of four and a half by Loch Kinellan
and the moor. Just beneath the falls the river is
spanned by an airy suspension bridge, from which a

good view is obtained. The graceful birches and lichen-covered boulders and the brown waters of the river—magnificent in spat—are the chief beauties of Rogie. Visitors often picnic here, and watch the salmon with their strange instinct of attainment, leaping in the falls.

Following the road beyond Rogie (the old coach route to the west coast) very charming views of the winding Blackwater are obtained. Four miles beyond the falls is **Loch Garve,** along the edge of which the carriage road and railway together wend. With timid horses it is therefore desirable to watch the time of trains. On the further side of the loch is situated Strathgarve House (C. A. Hanbury, Esq.). Following the road or railway, the next station beyond Garve is Loch Luichart, also in exquisite birchen scenery. Overlooking this loch, where the osprey and the eagle in their seasons may be seen, is Lady Ashburton's Loch Luichart Lodge, with its charming towers and terraces half hidden in the trees. In the forests above, the Deer (Red and Roe and Fallow) abound, and in winter come down to the low ground and even to the houses in search of food.

Leaving the Rogie road at the Achilty Inn, a very beautiful drive is along the side of **Loch Achilty** to Little Scatwell and the **Falls of Conan** (nine miles from the Spa). The former is said to be in point of beauty the most remarkable piece of water in the district. The hills are wooded to the water's edge as at Grasmere. A writer at the end of last century points out " no visible running water issues from this loch," which " certainly discharges

itself by subterranean passages" into the river. He
also speaks of an artificial island (as at Kinellan), a
place made for safety, "where the ruins of a house and
garden are still to be seen."

The road undulates beyond Achilty, passing the Lily
Loch, famous for its water-borne blooms; and winding
amid woods and rocks to the riverside at Little Scatwell.
Here carriages wait, while the excursion (another mile)
to the Falls of Conan is completed on foot. A short
additional walk brings one to the end of Loch Luichart,
and from this point the ascent (1,900 feet) may be made
of Sgurr Maire, a good botanical habitat. A short distance below Little Scatwell the river can be forded
unless the water be high, and the return journey
pleasantly varied by taking the road from Strath Conan.
In this stream rather fine pearls are to be obtained.

Yet other "falls," to which driving excursions are
often made, are the **Falls of Orrin** (nine miles by road)
on the estate of Fairburn (J. Stirling Esq.). The route
is by the village of Contin, and crosses the Conan by the
Moy Bridge. The Falls are situated on the left of the
carriage drive about a quarter of a mile within the lodge
gates. The rocky bed of the Orrin is here conglomerate,
and curiously water-worn. The stream rushes through
a very narrow channel, plunging into a deep pool
beneath. There are some deep circular holes in the
rock, worn (as at the Falls of the Beauly river at
Kilmorack) by the continual action of loose stones.
The drive to Fairburn House is marked "Private," but

Mr. Stirling kindly allows visitors to drive past the house on Tuesdays and Thursdays. The circuit is a wide one, and affords an uncommonly fine view. The ancient Tower, or Castle-keep, of Fairburn on the right-hand side of the drive will attract the attention of the antiquarian. It is reached by a footpath through the wood nearly opposite the Falls. The Spa invalid also may be interested to learn that in the woods beyond the House sulphur springs have been discovered, similar to, although much weaker than, the waters of Strathpeffer.

Scatwell, the **Meig**, and **Strath Conan** (seventeen miles).—Only firstrate pedestrian powers, or a pair of good horses, can comfortably accomplish this distance from the Spa ; but for natural grandeur of scenery the drive is perhaps unsurpassed in the country. Crossing the Conan at Moy, the road slowly mounts with the river. Above Scatwell House (the residence of C. Bell, Esq.) commences the wilder country of Strath Conan. Leaving Scatwell, sheltered by its tall pines, behind, the road climbs a long steep hill. From here onwards it follows the course of the Meig. In winter a torrent, this stream is thrown into a series of cataracts tumbling down the bottom of a deep gorge. From the brink of the chasm one can gain a glimpse of the waters, more than two hundred feet below. This extraordinary gorge is about a mile in length, and from it the troubled waters flow forth to join the sister stream from the Loch Luichart at Little Scatwell in the plain below. Eight miles farther on, at the very head of the Strath, is Strath Conan Lodge, a residence of the Right Hon. A. J. Balfour, M.P., set in the hilly haunt of golden eagles.

Brahan Castle.—A favourite circular drive of thirteen or fourteen miles is by way of Contin to Brahan Castle (six miles from the Spa), returning through the village of Maryburgh and Dingwall to the valley of Strathpeffer. The carriage road from Contin follows the Conan, passes the Moy Bridge (the route to Orrin, and Fairburn, Scatwell, and Strath Conan) and divides about a mile short of the castle. Here a monument marks the spot where the sister of the late Honourable Mrs. Stewart Mackenzie met with a fatal carriage accident. This has been generally interpreted as a fulfilment of a prophecy of the Brahan Seer (Coinneach Odhar). The right-hand road conducts to the castle, whilst the road to the left, mounting a little, skirts the beautiful woods of Brahan. Fragments have fallen from the cliffs above, and, covered with moss and ferns, form a magnificent natural rockery. Here the botanist will love to linger, for "the world is all before him where to choose"— from the crevices of the Brahan Cliffs to the reedy margins of Loch Ussie. The castle is a massive square building, and was once strongly fortified. It contains some fine works of art. The flower gardens are beautifully laid out by the design of Sir Joseph Paxton. Visitors are permitted to visit the grounds and castle on Tuesdays and Fridays.

Falls of Kilmorack, on the Beauly river.—* "The Falls of Kilmorack, two miles from Beauly, may either be driven to all the way, or train may be taken to Beauly (thirteen miles). The drive is by Moy Bridge and Marybank, beyond which fine views are obtained on the left, of Brahan Castle and its surroundings. On the plain of the Muir of Ord are two upright stone pillars, commemorative of some feat of ancient warfare. The Falls lie west from Beauly, and are reached by way of Beauly Bridge. They are situated immediately underneath the parish church of Kilmorack, and are less remarkable for their height than their breadth and quantity of water, and for the accompaniments of lofty rocks, smooth green banks, and hanging woods which encircle them. The river, dashing from between two lofty precipices, where it is confined to an extremely narrow channel, suddenly expands into an open semicircular basin, through which it slowly glides, and is then precipitated over its lower edge in a series of small cataracts. Below the Falls on the right bank of the stream Beaufort Castle (Lord Lovat) is seen to great advantage. A fine view may be had from a bridge across the river, two or three hundred yards below the Falls. Another group of waterfalls occurs about three miles farther up the river, at the top of a romantic ride called 'The Drhuim,' which signifies a narrow pass. This is the most typically Highland and beautiful part of the

---

* Extracted by permission from the late Dr. Manson's book.

course of the Beauly river. On either hand the mountain
acclivities are rather steep and rocky, and the valley
between them is not a quarter of a mile broad; but
woods of birch and fir encompass the whole scene,
especially on the north side, and the edges of the river
are fringed with rows of oak, weeping birches, and
alders. In one part, half up the Strath, near the cottage
of Teanassie (the burn of which will reward the
explorer) the waters plunge through a rocky passage
encircling high pyramids of stone, standing up in the
midst of the stream, gigantic witnesses of its ceaseless
and consuming power. On the southern bank, on a
high conical mound, rising above a perpendicular sheet
of rock, is Dun Fion, a vitrified structure, laid open
some years ago for the inspection of the curious.

" At the farther end of the Drhuim, the road begins
to ascend towards the interior of the country, and here
the river is seen pouring down on each side of a high
rounded hill, covered with oak and birch, at the lower
extremity of which it forms the second set of small but
beautiful cataracts. This is the island of Aigas (for the
river parts into two, and encircles it), with a picturesque
shooting-lodge, which was the summer retreat of the late
Sir Robert Peel, during the last year of the great
statesman's life. An open glen succeeds, with the
house of Aigas (J. W. Gordon Oswald, Esq.) on the
right; on the left the elegant mansion of Eskadale (a
shooting-lodge of Lord Lovat's); to the westward, the
small hamlet of Wester Eskadale, behind which, though

half-concealed by the birch trees, appear the white walls
and pinnacles of a handsome Roman Catholic Chapel
built by Lord Lovat, where may be seen the tombs of
the Chevaliers d'Albany, the 'Sobieski-Stuarts.' Four
miles on, is Erchless Castle, a stately old tower modern-
ized, the seat of ' The Chisholm.' At Eskadale there is
a ferry across the river, of which the pedestrian visitor
to the Falls and the Drhuim might avail himself to vary
the homeward route to Beauly—returning by a road
which runs along the south side of the river. About
a mile beyond Erchless are Struy Bridge and Inn. The
drive from Beauly to Struy Bridge, up the one side of
the stream and down the other, may be easily managed
between an up-train in the morning and a down-train in
the afternoon. More picturesque scenery than that
along the course of the Beauly is rarely to be met with
in the Highlands. Time permitting, the ruins of the
ancient Cistercian Priory of Beauly, founded A.D. 1230,
by John Bisset, of Lovat, might be inspected.

" On the course of the Glass (the continuation upwards
of the Beauly), and between Fasnakyle Bridge (ten miles
above Struy) and Loch Benneveian (five miles farther
on) is ' The Chisholm's Pass,' the scenery of which is
somewhat similar to the celebrated birken bowers of
Killiecrankie and the Trossachs, but on a much ampler
and grander scale. In ascending the shelving opening
(by the road on the north side of the stream), a prolonged vista, in one general mantle of foliage, rising
high on either side, forms a woodland picture of incom-

parable beauty, threaded by the rocky channel of the river. The road, on the south side of the stream, from Fasnakyle Bridge to Guisachan, the picturesque Highland residence of Lord Tweedmouth, runs within a mile of the pass on the right.

"**The Black Rock.**—A very extraordinary and interesting natural curiosity, and one well worthy of a visit, is what is called 'The Black Rock,' a frightful chasm, occurring in a thick level bed of conglomerate near Evantown on the Cromarty Firth. It is twelve miles from the Spa, and may either be driven to all the way, or train may be taken to Novar Station. If a carriage be taken, the drive along the margin of the Cromarty Firth will be much enjoyed. A branch road, striking off northwards from the main road, just beyond Evantown, brings us in a mile near to the chasm. Only eight feet wide, and in many places arched over by intermingling branches of trees from the opposite sides, it is 200 feet in depth, and about two miles in length. At its bottom, the waters of the Aultgraat or *terrific burn*, visible only here and there from the bank above, rush and tumble, and boom, and thunder down deep in subterranean gloom, fit haunt for goblin grim. A footpath along the wooded bank conducts, a mile and a quarter upwards, to a wooden bridge over the chasm, from which (if the beholder will venture) an open view of its profundity may be obtained. The Aultgraat issues from Loch Glass, about three miles above the chasm, and forms, after quitting the loch, a series of highly

8

picturesque falls. Loch Glass lies at the base of Ben
Wyvis. The chasm is evidently the result of the action
of the water on the rock, mostly, perhaps, at a time
when the conglomerate was in a less compact state
than now.*

"**Cromarty.**—At Invergordon, three miles beyond
Alness, there is a ferry to the Cromarty side of the
firth. This is a pleasant and convenient route for
visiting the native place of Hugh Miller. A conveyance,
running between the landing-point and Cromarty, in
connection with the mail train passing Invergordon,
leaves the Balblair ferry (excepting Sundays) at 2 P.M.
The distance to Cromarty from the ferry is eight miles.
Carriages may also be obtained at Balblair Inn.

"**Dunrobin Castle.**—With the recent railway extension, Dunrobin Castle, the magnificent residence of the
Duke of Sutherland, near Golspie, is now within easy
reach of Strathpeffer. The scenery of the Sutherland part
of the journey will be much enjoyed. The castle was
founded by Robert, second Earl of Sutherland, A.D. 1079,
and by recent additions has become 'one of the most
princely palaces in the kingdom, and undoubtedly one
of the largest in Scotland.' The private rooms are
arranged into numerous suites of apartments, each
appropriated to some member of the family, and named
accordingly, as the Argyle, the Blantyre, and other

---

* Of course such places have in the north their legends. See
Hugh Miller's *Scenes and Legends of the North of Scotland*, p. 171 ;
also, *Rambles of a Geologist*, p. 335.

apartments, and distinguished by its own peculiar style, coloured decorations, and paintings. The state-rooms specially prepared for Her Majesty, command the grand sea-ward view, comprehending almost the entire circuit of the Moray Firth. They are, of course, furnished in the most sumptuous manner, as are also the other public and principal private rooms. Admission is liberally granted to the castle and grounds.

"The late Mr. Frank Buckland, in his *Log Book of a Fisherman and Zoologist,* remarks :—'A museum situated in the pleasure-grounds near the castle is admirably fitted up, and contains a most interesting collection. The antiquities, especially the Pictish relics, are well worthy of notice, but to the naturalist the collection of birds is of the highest interest. In the museum we find specimens of nearly all the native *avi-fauna* in Scotland.'

"Mr. Buckland goes on to say that ' there is perhaps no district in the Highlands where the breed of wild cats exists in greater purity or perfection than in Suther-landshire. . . . Tradition has it that once upon a time Sutherland was invaded by a hostile band, and that upon landing they were opposed by an advanced guard of furious wild cats, and so well did the latter defend the coast that the enemy skedaddled without coming to the scratch ! '

" **Battlefield of Culloden.**—A very interesting excursion might be made by railway to Culloden Moor, the scene of the last battle on British soil, where Prince Charles

Stuart, after having penetrated into the heart of England, and imperilled the existence of the Hanoverian dynasty, was at last defeated by the Duke of Cumberland, and the hopes of the house of Stuart finally extinguished, April 16th, 1746. Culloden Station is three and a quarter miles from Inverness, and the battle-field about three from the station. A monumental tumulus or obelisk on the heath, abandoned after being barely commenced, marks the spot where the contest was fiercest ; and the public road passes through the graves of the slain, which consist of two or three grass-covered mounds. The ash-tree, whence Prince Charles beheld the battle, still stands, the best part of a mile to the west ; and the less perishable boulder-stone, from which, it is said, the Duke of Cumberland issued his orders, is shown on the roadside, about a quarter of a mile east from the principal heap of graves. About 1,200 men are said to have perished in the battle, the number of killed on both sides being about equal."

West Coast and **Islands**.—These are readily accessible from Strathpeffer by the Dingwall and Skye Railway.

CHAPTER X.

STRATHPEFFER is separated from the valley of the Conan by a sharp and narrow ridge, running north-east and south-west, and terminating at either extremity in a bluff and almost precipitous hill. At the western end of this ridge, which is popularly known as the *Cat's Back*, is Cnoc Moir (representing the Cat's Head), a wood-covered elevation of 882 feet; whilst at the eastern or seaward end, Knock Farril (579 feet) rises abruptly from the low alluvial plain. The summit is nearly a mile and a half from the Spa, and three and a half from the sea, and situated in a direct line between the two. The pedestrian, ascending behind the Ben Wyvis Hotel, or taking the lower road by the Peffery, traverses the fir-wood on the side of the ridge, and, by an easy ascent, soon reaches the depression or pass which marks the neck of Knock Farril. From this point, which is the point of access, the hill rises steep on all sides and almost vertical along the northern face. Here for a length of about one hundred feet the conglomerate

rock of the hill juts out as a bare cliff. These rugged
sides are topped by a nearly level oval, measuring about
one hundred and fifty yards in length by a third as much
in breadth. Within this space the grass is ever rich
and green;* here, in one spot are the remains of an
old well, about which tradition states that when the
stone shutting it down is lifted, the water will bubble
up and fill the valley. Here, also, around the oval
are huge blocks, once a complete line of ramparts,
compacted together of half-molten stones.

This is the famous *Vitrified Fort* of Knock Farril,
probably the finest specimen of its kind in Scotland.
These structures have long been a source of perplexity
to the antiquary. The exact mode of their formation in
ancient times must probably be counted among the
perished arts. A careful examination of the semi-fused
or vitrified mass shows it to be composed of the
elements of the native conglomerate. No doubt a flux,
perhaps vegetable ash, was used, and by its aid some of

---

* "The summits and sides of those hills, which were occupied
by our ancestors as *hill forts* usually exhibit a far richer herbage
than corresponding heights in the neighbourhood, with the mineral
soil derived from the same source. It is to be kept in view that
these positions of strength were at the same time occupied as
hill folds, into which, during the threatened or actual invasion of
the district by a hostile tribe, the cattle were driven, especially
during the night, as to places of safety, and sent out to pasture
during the day. And the droppings of these collected herds would,
as takes place in analogous cases at present, speedily improve
the soil to such an extent as to induce a permanent fertility."
—DR. FLEMING, *Zoology of the Bass.*

the material is completely fused, whilst other portions
are much less affected. The vitrifying agent was, of
course, intense heat. It is still uncertain whether the
vitrification extends completely through the enormous
masses of the ramparts. The author has had an opportunity of examining a section of the formation where the
ground had at one place given way and fallen in (*vide
infra*). Underneath were rounded stones and angular
fragments, entirely unaffected by heat : a little nearer the
surface there were similar stones, but bent and untorted
(when softened by heat) from the pressure of neighbouring stones, and in some cases adherent one to another
by an incomplete and superficial fusion of their edges.
Then above these he found the true vitrification, cellular
like pumice, or streaked and glazed like the slag from
an iron furnace—the whole formation forcibly suggesting
a piecrust, compacted by heat and stretched over the
loose material underneath. It is, therefore, quite evident
that the operation of heat was *from the surface*, and not
as was once supposed, from internal volcanic sources.
That wood was employed in the original process seems
also certain ; for Hugh Miller found fragments of
charcoal embedded in detached blocks, and the late Dr.
Manson made the same discovery in connection with the
small vitrified structures (three in number) on Sgurr
Maire near Scatwell.

Among several explanatory theories the most probable
one seems to be that the fort was originally constructed
in very early times, of *loose stones* only, as a place of

defence and refuge. At the same time, the commanding position of the hill, with that of many ·others in the Highlands, made them well fitted for Beacon stations.* According to Sir George Mackenzie, after the defeat of the Picts by the Scots in the eighth century, nearly twenty of these stations were in use in the great valley extending from Fort Augustus to Dingwall and Banff. According to this view, then, the use of beacon fires, acting by chance on some favourable combination of stones with flux, would on some occasion have taught the secret of vitrification. This discovery the inhabitants would be glad to apply on a larger scale to works of fortification, some of them in places where it is nearly certain beacon fires can never have been used.

Some appearances within the ramparts at Knock Farril have suggested to the author that the fort may very probably have provided *covered* shelter in the shape of large caverns, roofed over with a crust of vitrified stone. Remembering the appearances of the section of surface above referred to, this does not seem a very improbable supposition. Moreover, the ground has sunk deeply in many places, and the smoke of a fire may actually be made to travel underground from one hole to another. The matter needs further investigation, but should this surmise prove correct, the Fort of Knock Farril must indeed have been a masterpiece of defensive art.

* Cnoc Fallerie or Fairilees, Gaelic words, signifying *The Hill of the Watching Fort.*

Another explanation is furnished by Hugh Miller in his *Scenes and Legends*, and must not be too hastily set aside. "On the summit of Knock Farril are the remains of a vitrified fort which was originally constructed, says tradition, by a gigantic tribe of *Fions*, for the protection of their wives and children when they themselves were engaged in hunting. It chanced in one of their excursions that a mean-spirited little fellow of the party, not much more than fifteen feet in height, was so distanced by his more active brethren, that leaving them to follow out the chase he returned home, and throwing himself down, much fatigued, on the side of the eminence, fell fast asleep. Garry, for so the unlucky hunter was called, was no favourite with the women of the tribe;—he was spiritless and diminutive and ill-tempered; and as they could make little else of him that they cared for, they converted him into the butt of many a joke and the sport of many a humour. On seeing that he had fallen asleep, they stole out to where he lay, and after fastening his long hair with pegs to the grass, awakened him with their shouts and laughter. He strove to extricate himself, but in vain; until at length, infuriated by their gibes and the pain of his own exertions, he wrenched up his head leaving half his locks behind him, and hurrying after them, set fire to the stronghold into which they had rushed for shelter. The flames rose till they mounted over the roof, and broke out at every slit and opening; but Garry, unmoved by the shrieks and groans of the sufferers within, held fast the door until all was silent ; when he fled into the remote Highlands towards the west. The males of the tribe, who had, meanwhile been engaged in hunting on that part of the northern Sutor which bears the name of the Hill of Nigg, alarmed by the vast column of smoke which they saw ascending from their dwelling, came pressing on to the Firth of Cromarty, and leaping across on their hunting spears, they hurried home. But they arrived to find only a huge pile of embers, fanned by the breeze, and amid which the very stones of the building were sputtering and bubbling with the intense heat, like the contents of a boiling cauldron. Wild with rage and astonishment, and yet collected enough to conclude that none but Garry could be the author of a deed so barbarous, they tracked him into a nameless Highland glen, which has ever since been known as Glen-*Garry*, and there tore him to pieces. And as all the women of the tribe perished in the flames, there was an end, when this forlorn and widowed generation had passed away, to the whole race of the *Fions*."

We may conclude this chapter with an extract from a modern legend, contributed by an intellectual Fion, who came lately a visitor to Strathpeffer, hunting with his long spear.

KNOCK FARRIL.

There is a Bay on Scotia's eastern shores,
Its wide blue waters parted by an isle
Into two Firths, which deep the mainland cleave.
The northern inlet to a Valley leads,

Once full of reeds and marshes, and its sides
Clad with primæval Forest, now strewn o'er
With smiling field and hamlet, close-set copse.
And the white cottages of Crofters. set
Each in its patch of green, upon the hills.
Above them stretches moorland as of yore,
Heather and fern and waste of treeless bog,
With many a craggy boulder scarred by time,
And massy smooth rock-surface, glacier-worn.

In this wide Vale, a narrow Ridge of Hill
Stretches toward the sea, its steep sides girt
With pines and firs in frowning dark array.
At the sea end the hill-top sinks abrupt,
Leaving a Summit, bare of tree or shrub,
Craggy and sharp-descending every side.
O'erlooked from here, the smooth and land-locked Firth
Is seen a few miles distant, and of old
The Norsemen's long low barks might be descried,
As to these shores they ploughed their stealthy way.
Hence Pictish men in ages long ago,
Here placed their Fort, and deep in vitreous walls
Entrenched secure a camp, the sheer hillside
And rocky rampart yielding good defence.
Still tread we o'er their hard-burned glassy stones,
Now grass-grown, softened by the hand of Time,
Who loves to spread the silken veil of Peace
Upon the ruins of the strife of men.

Knock Farril is the name the headland bears.
And so its summit seems to cleave the air,
Aspiring to be peer of heights around,
As some wee sister to the Matterhorn
Or monarch peak among the snowy Alps.
The eye that gazes towards the horizon's marge
Beholds the forms of Mountains all around.
Hill behind hill, they rise in rugged shapes.
Here Wyvis with his sons, o'ertopping all,

Rounded and vast, the summit hid in cloud.
Behind, the steeper mountains which enclose
Lochs not a few, and in the distance far
Scuir Vullen's twin-shaped peaks, a landmark plain.

Here late I wandered, pilgrim of the Earth
Scaled the hillside and on the lonely top
Stood long in thought. . . . The western squall had hung
His heavy drapery o'er the northern hills,
Black glowered the storm-cloud o'er Inchvannie's Heights,
And through the mists and rain Ben Wyvis showed
But a faint vision of his awful form.

The everlasting hills surrounded me.
The inconstant heavens played o'er hill and dale
In sunny smile, or frowning storm again,
Or rain's mild influence, but the mountain shapes
Abide unchanged, their outline rough and bare
The same as eke it was in ancient days,
When hardy Picts their darksome forests tracked,
And watched the shining Firth from this same hill :
The same as when Mackenzie of Kintail
Lord of Kinellan's Isle, upon this ridge
O'ercame proud Munro, and in yonder Strath
Set up, in memory, the Eagle Stone.*

   *   *   *   *   *   *   *

* *Vide* section Antiquities.

CHAPTER XI.

BEN WYVIS.

OME jottings of a recent ascent of the Ben may perhaps be allowed to take the place of a more general description.*

Early in September a party of seven set out to make the ascent of Ben Wyvis. For days we had watched the thick covering of clouds resting on the broad hilltop, until it was feared we should have to give up the expedition. But at length one morning the mist began to roll away. Our spirits rose : the party was summoned, and we prepared to go. Sandwiches were hastily packed up, strong boots and clothing suitable

---

* The distance to the top of the Ben is about ten miles. It is well to employ a guide, and few are more communicative than George Munro, of Park, who knows the track very well. Another guide is Simon McKay, of Auchterneed. Ponies may be taken all the way to the top. A splendid prospect may be enjoyed by ascending the hill about midnight and watching the sunrise from the summit. Otherwise, one should leave the Spa shortly after breakfast.

for a day's rough walking were put on, and we were ready to start. Each one carried a small basket, a walking stick, and a light woollen wrap for cold breezes on the top, and for halts by the way.

Some had driven to Auchterneed to save their strength for the climb. We joined company there, and, though rather late in the day (we left the Strath at noon), began the ascent in good spirits. For the first mile or two the sun beat hotly on our heads, but one of us suggested the device of placing cool cabbage-leaves in our hats. These we obtained from a cottage garden near the route, and found them very grateful. The summer had been a wet one, and the road above the railway station was in bad condition. It had recently been overflowed by a small stream, and was still very muddy, but we soon got beyond this, on to the muir. About a mile above the station, our guide pointed out to us the remarkable **Cupped Stone** which lies quite close to the pathway. It is dotted over with numerous cuplike depressions, the origin of which has been a subject of conjecture to the lover of antiquities. Some believe that it was employed as an altar for sacrifice to the heathen deities. A mile or more above the stone, we traversed the peat-fields, where the operation of cutting and drying " peats " may be seen. Here the road became more winding and uncertain, and we thought of shortening it by passing through the heather. Taking various ways we at length regained the road, discovering in this case as in so many others, that our " short cut " had been a long one.

About here we made our first halt for rest and refresh-
ment, choosing for shelter a high bank beside a stream.
This stream was henceforward our companion for a
good part of the way.

Soon after this, the real hill-climb began, but the toil
of this was much lightened by the lovely views of the
country around, now gradually unfolded before us. It
must be confessed that at this point we stopped to
admire the scenery very frequently indeed !

Still up we went—not a very steep climb, but a
continuous one, straight up the side of the Ben. On,
and yet on, sometimes picking a bright scarlet leaf of
the little tormentil or a shaded red one of the rarer
nut-berry, or looking for some of the long trailing deer's
grass, so abundant on the Inchvannie heights below.
We traversed the side of the Horse Hill, now so mourn-
fully associated with the tragic incident of a year or
two ago. Here the hill got steeper, and afforded a fine
view of the mountain Pass between Little and Greater
Wyvis. Through this Pass at one time lay a chief
route to the west coast. We were now nearing our
camping ground, the fountain-head of water from which
the houses of Strathpeffer are supplied. As we
approached it our way took a more easterly and circuitous
direction, terminating in a huge bank of brown peaty
soil, over which we scrambled. Above this, amid patches
of green, was the clear crystal spring. Here we rested,
as the custom is, for about half an hour, and took our
repast with draughts of the cool water.

From here our way led along the top of the huge
mountain by an easy slope of delightfully springy turf.
Following the wire-fence, a narrow path, and one that
would be dangerous in mist, conducted round the edge
of a large Corrie. (This Corrie has obtained its name
Corie-na-Feol, or the Flesh Corrie, from the number of
deer killed by falling over its precipitous sides.) Thus
we reached the huge cairn which is placed on the
highest point of the hill.

From here the view is magnificent. Range beyond
range of hills stretch in almost endless array as far as
the eye can reach. Not, for the most part, jagged and
peaked and stern, like the cliffs of Arran and Skye,
but gently rounded and smooth like the swelling waves of
the sea. Ross and Sutherland, Inverness-shire, Cromarty,
portions of eight counties it is said, may be seen, with
innumerable lochs and the blue waters of the Cromarty
and Moray Firths lying far below. Then the air—
how fresh and exhilarating! As one of the party
remarked, one could walk miles without fatigue on
the top of Ben Wyvis.

But we must not linger long, for the sun is already
sinking behind the hills, and rosy clouds fringe the sky.
The descent was easy at first, but ere we had gained
the beaten track it was almost dark, and we plunged
along our rather uncertain way, with occasional shouts
of merriment as one and another tripped in the heather
or stumbled in the bog. Then the moon rose, and
greatly enhanced, by her weird silver light, the charm of

the scene. Just before gaining the road above the station we were struck by a rather peculiar atmospheric effect. Little gusts of *hot* air blew across us several times, and were noticed by all our party.

We reached Strathpeffer about eight o'clock, not over-tired, even the ladies, by our twenty miles of mountaineering.

BEN WYVIS: THE MOUNTAIN OF STORM.

A TRUE TALE OF MICKLE DREAD.*

(1) *Prelude.*

HE air is heavy with a sense of coming change : safe to their roosts the birdies hie : the beasties to their holes in the heathy banks. Silence reigns in the air—a short-lived calm. Light rain is pattering on tree and grass.

See from the west it cometh ! I hear the far-off roar of the Storm Cloud ! Nearer and nearer it cometh. The groaning pines are waiting the onset ; nearer and nearer it cometh, in fitful gust, rising and falling, swelling and dying away ; struggling as it were to be free, chafing its chains and its shackles, gathering its force with roar of defiance ; sighing again, lingering on mountain and valley.

Ha ! it is here ! Blast of the ocean, booming and bellowing, raging in fury ; crashing the pine-woods, thundering like demon let loose 'mongst the dwellings of men ; shaking the house to its base, rending asunder the tree of the forest, tearing its roots from the rock,

---

* Kindly contributed by the anonymous " Fion " already referred to, to whom the author would again offer his grateful acknowledg ments.

bearing before it destruction and terror. Such is the Tempest; such is the breath of the Storm.

It is passed; it is over. Only the gusts of the breeze play upon us, mournful, uncertain, wailing and pleading; mimicking feebly the Storm Blast they follow: uttering, muttering, dying away, dying o'er hill and o'er dale. Softly repeating, renewing, advancing, falling again to a sigh, gliding away, falling away. While from the Storm Cloud, torrents of raindrops pour on the landscape. Nature is weeping: Nature is mourning the deeds of the Tempest; soothing her children, filling their treasuries, building up fresh, new Life, on the *Wreck of the Storm.*

(2) *The Storm.*

It was winter. The snow lay thick on the higher slopes of the king of Ross-shire mountains. Few or none brave its snows and its storms in the long Highland winter. The shepherds tend their flocks on the lower heights; the crofter has fetched all his peat in summer. Only the deer, roaming in the forest glens, share with the alpine hares and the eagle an unchallenged sovereignty. It was afternoon on a latter day in February when a single traveller was seen wending his way through the heights of Inchvannie. He was a young man, in tourist dress, slender in build and stature. Asking a crofter as he passed the way to Ben Wyvis, he was warned that the hour was late, the short winter day was waning, and it was now unsafe to tempt the

storms of the mountain. And so he passed on, and the
crofter thought no more of the wayside pilgrim. But
the pilgrim heeded not the words of counsel—or heeded
them all too well! Alas, poor wanderer! the storm for
thee has gathered; the sullen clouds have hid the face
of thy heaven; the low rumble of no earthly thunder
has sounded in thy ears; the fortress of the soul is
tottering to its base : it needeth but the lightning flash
to lay thee low.

He hath toiled up the shoulder of the steep ascent,
long past the topmost cotter's hut; the fir-trees are left
far below ; and now he is crossing the snowy moorland,
which lies around the base of the great mountain—a
waste of moss and heathy bog; his feet sink in the crisp
black peat. Mile after mile is passed ; the sun is tending
to the western hills ; that sun, now hid by clouds,
which he shall see no more. Alas, poor wanderer !
storm-tossed wanderer! knowest thou not the sun is
behind those clouds ? Life is not always winter ;—
he that hath courage to endure shall overcome ! Where
are the dreams of thy youth; the hopes of early days,
the love of brother and of sister ; the delights of this fair
world ? Alas, the sullen storm hath gathered ! All is
hid ! And now the boggy upland, clad in its garment of
pure white snow, is crossed, and the traveller turns to
breast the steep ascent. 'Tis a rough mountain-side,
strewn with grey boulders, bracken and heather spring-
ing all around. He climbs higher, higher, over the
wide vale below, and ever as he mounts the distant hill

outline, dim in mist, still rises around him. And now
he has chosen a nook beside a rock and lays him down.
Alas, poor wanderer, here in this wild where no eye—
save One—can see thee, dim in the mists of this mountain
of storm, the greatest storm of all is within thine own
breast! Hast thou no thought of a Father Who loveth
thee? Where is thy faith? Must love and hope be all
quenched? Is there none to whisper a word in thine
ear; to uphold thy tottering reason; to lift the black
veil of despair? Is there no comforter? The clouded
sun sinks low, the storm is dark as night.

     *   *   *   *   *

Hark, what was that sound methought I heard high up
on Wyvis' slopes? 'Twas not the cry of the moor-bird,
or the bleating of a strayed sheep; it echoed from peak
to peak, till it was lost in the ravines. 'Tis over : all is
still; save only the sighing of the wind upon the heather,
and the drifting snow. All is still, and Nature is at
peace,—but a soul hath burst unbidden the veil of the
eternal world.

(3) *The Wreck.*

The long, long winter is over. Hail to the glad Spring,
unlocking frozen waters, and making the whole earth to
leap forth in bud and bloom. Now are the sheep led
again to higher pastures; now again the crofter driveth
his slow wain up to the boggy moorland around the
mount of storms, that he may lade it with peat and
rushes. It is evening of a day in May. The tramp of

constables is heard drawing nigh to the dwelling of the
medical officer, with summons requiring him to proceed
forthwith up Ben Wyvis, there to inspect, examine and
report touching the body of a man unknown.   It wants
little more than an hour of sunset, yet delay to the
morrow is not suffered, albeit three long months hath
the mountain waited to give up its dead.   The day, the
hour, is come ; this night it must be done.   They set off
therefore on foot, slowly climbing up the hill ; they
have halted here and there to impress a horse from the
crofters' huts, and now they are all mounted, and the
cavalcade winds up the slopes, and across the wide
upland wet with winter rains.

Shepherds and gamekeepers join them as they go
along, for the news of the wanderer's fate has stirred the
whole country-side.   The sun is set, and the shades of
evening have begun to fall, when they draw nigh to the
spot, and descry up the steep hillside above them that
for which they have come.   A creeping sense of weari-
ness and dread steals over the bravest of the band, and
a halt is called to rest and refresh their souls.   And
now they go to their work.   'Tis a weird scene in the
twilight.   A group of swart Highlanders stand around
in plaid and cloak; and in the midst, couched in his
lowly bed of fern and heather, the lifeless corse.
Above, below, as far as eye can reach, the wide waste
of mountain and moorland.

And this was once a fellow-man of hopes and fears like
ours !   He lies as though at rest, his feet crossed, his

head laid upon hat and headgear in a nook between two
stones. The fingers of the right hand still clasp the
weapon whose leaden missile has ploughed the brain.
Three months have done their work upon his shrunken
features and sightless balls. They search his clothing.
Watch : no lack of gold ; two common lead-pencils,
worn to the stump ; but no shred of paper, no letter, no
book,—nothing which would lend a clue to the wanderer's name. Nor could the slightest clue be found.
Had he hidden his papers in the cairn of stones on the
top of the peak ? The cairn is searched in vain. All
is unknown. His name and lineage, his connections,
dwelling-place, calling—all are hid. Too surely has the
poor wanderer buried all trace of these : and himself
laid in depth of winter, high on a lone Scotch mountain.
That shattered brain—did it own a trained intellect, a
mind of culture and research ? Methinks there is a
trait of genius, though it be a genius gone astray, in
his choice of such a death—alone in Nature's solitude,
where none should find him until hope of recognition
was all past.

And so they bore him from his mountain bed, poor
waif of human-kind ! across the heath, and down the long
and winding track, the selfsame pathway he had trodden,
instinct with life, albeit self-sentenced unto death, three
months before. And they laid him where "after life's
fitful fever he sleeps." Nigh to a low stone wall, the
nameless wanderer's grave is hidden by nettles, and
the long rank grass : no stone is raised above it, but

He that keepeth the Books, He knoweth where he lies.

(4) *The Pilgrimage.*

Spring blossomed into summer. The purple heather now clothes the brae, the pride of Scotia's hills. From their covert in the fern and ling upstarting, grouse and ptarmigan cleave the startled air. The rushing burns have dwindled to small brooks : the soft crisp moss rebounds from the passing tread. Two tall forms in tourist guise are seen climbing slowly the steep heights above the Skye railway. In the rich carpeting of heather and bracken they have found the beech-fern and the oak-fern, gentian and fragrant bog-myrtle, and the shining green leaves of the bear-berry. Heedless of rain, they have mounted now the shoulder of the hill, and struck into a rugged peat track. The club moss lifts its spikes of fruit, and winds its snaky shoots beside the path.

The track is followed until it is seen no longer, and now we are out upon the open moorland among the mountain heights. We have far out-topped the familiar summits of the Strath. Craig Ulladaile has sunk low ; the Raven Rock is scarcely seen ; Tor Achilty is dwarfed ; the Cat's Back is far below the horizon. Around us rise the giants of the forest, Ben Wyvis and his sons, all owning Gaelic names of uncouth sound. There is not a hut or sign of life in all the landscape, save a few heaps of peat and white-faced sheep upon the further hills. 'Tis weary work plodding over the rough bog ; the sun, too, is near its setting ; the heights are clothed in mist. We have no path, it is easy to get lost on this wide, sloping bog—to mistake the landmarks and be overtaken by the night.

We make for a large granite boulder, which rears itself alone upon the wide expanse ; and, clambering up, sit there awhile. All else is wet with rain. There with compass and map the route is fixed. It is up the valley to the left of a bare hill. Following for a mile or two the friendly guidance of the new-laid watercourse, we found ourselves at the foot of the summit. It was verging on twilight, but a strange longing led us on to seek the spot where the wanderer had died. We climb from knoll to knoll, and stone to stone, startling the sheep from their pasturage, until we reach a small eminence some half way up. A good-sized boulder, grey with lichen, lies athwart the slope, a smaller one at the end ;—some heather and ling peep out from their edges, green with Nature's freshness. Here he lay ;—his last look fell on yonder summits, cleft by a deep ravine ; the dense mist, ragged-edged, mantling, then perhaps as also now, around the peaks. . . .

Here we muse awhile, ere our steps turn homeward again into the battle of life ; muse over one who has fallen, who might not bear the ills of the way,—the storms which beat within and without ;—and who here, on the mountain of storms, lay struck by sore tempest of the soul. Nature meanwhile renews her life, covers age

and death by budding youth, and makes the sunshine of
a new spring to put to flight the mists of winter.
Wistfully, half in fear and half in hope, dare we peer
forward toward the farther shore where

Lands the voyager at last?

Shall there be no spring-tide birth to chase away the
winter-death, dire mist, and tempest? Man knoweth
not. In holier scales than those of earth are weighed
the good and evil of our lives. And who shall say the
bark that foundered in a hurricane were less seaworthy
than such as sail with colours flying beneath a summer
sky?

I have finished my tale. Let it tell not alone of
storm, but of peace; not alone of darkness but of light;
not alone of despair but of hope—hope that springeth
eternal; that seeth in Nature's bounty and renewal
the love of a Father; that layeth anchor in something
higher than the heavens, deeper than the depths. It is
a saying of Emerson: " We judge of a man's wisdom by
his HOPE."

CHAPTER XII.

(1) GEOLOGY.

STRATHPEFFER is situated on the *Old Red Sandstone* beds, a geologic formation laid down in salt seas abounding in fish. The larger hills, Ben Wyvis to the north, and the mountains of Ross to the west, are composed of the more ancient *Primary Rocks*—Gneiss (whinstone), with Mica and Quartz. From Craig Ulladaile, north-west of the Spa, eastwards to the Cat's Back and Knock Farril, the beds of the "Old Red" appear in ascending order— that is, those nearer the earth's surface to the eastward —forming parallel strips at the outcrop, with a general dip E.S.E. *Conglomerate* caps the series, forming a sharp ridge or knife-edge south of the valley, and terminated by the two abrupt summits known as Knock Farril and the Cat's Back. On the south aspect of the last-named hill, the cliffs of Brahan, with the broken masses at their base, admirably exhibit the pudding-like formation of this rock. To the west, the limit of the conglomerate formation extends as far as Tor Achilty.

It is well exposed in the precipitous eastern face of this hill.

Beyond this point even the outlines of the country testify to a different geologic structure. Mr. W. Hamilton Bell thus describes the prospect from the View Rock, about two miles west of the Spa: " You see the flat rolling hills of the gneiss in the Scatwell Hills to the south-west, and Ben Wyvis with his huge mass and elevation of 3,500 feet in the north ; the latter a true gneiss mountain, with breadth of shoulders and amplitude of base enough to serve a mountain thrice as tall ; but which, like all its congeners of this ancient formation, was arrested in its second stage of growth. Farther west, the mica hills of Scuir Vullin and Scuir-na-Vertach are seen, with their high sharp-peaked cones of 2,500 feet, so typical of that formation ; while in the far west rise the steep hills on the west side of Loch Carron with their abrupt but square tops of the quartz, and the red and purple stones of Applecross ; and again to the east the low-lying Old Red of the Black Isle running along the south side of the Cromarty Firth." He goes on to recommend, as full of geological interest, the walk, about three miles, across the hills from the View Rock to the Dingwall and Skye Railway : " The ground is not difficult, the rocks are mostly mica, which appears everywhere, and the formation is very well displayed both as to constituents and stratification, the dip and strike being almost everywhere well shown. The rocks themselves are well worth observation, being the Muscovite

Mica in large masses and nodules, mixed with the largest amount of garnets I have ever seen ; and at and near the Glenskiagh Cutting, the display of this most beautiful rock is quite wonderful."

The strata from which the Sulphur Waters take their origin appear in the bottom of the Strathpeffer valley. They vary in density and appearance from a loose brownish *shale* to a compact rock, or *breccia*, but all varieties are impregnated with a peculiar bituminous matter, and emit on fracture a somewhat fœtid odour of sulphuretted hydrogen. Hugh Miller, to whom all this district was familiar ground, thus describes the Strathpeffer rock. "It lies over that conglomerate member of the system, which, rising high in the Knock Farril range, forms the southern boundary of the valley and occupies the place of the lower ichthyolitic bed, so rich in organisms in various other parts of the country. But here the bed" [Sulphur-yielding Shales] "after it had been deposited in thin horizontal laminæ, and had hardened into stone, seems to have been broken up by some violent movement into minute sharpened fragments, that, without wear or attrition, were again consolidated into the *breccia* which it now forms. And its ichthyolites, if not previously absorbed, were probably destroyed in the convulsion. Detached scales and spines, however, if carefully sought for in the various openings of the valley, might still be found in the original laminæ of the fragments." [Mr. Miller himself found none.] "They must have been amazingly abundant in it once, for so largely saturated is the rock with the organic matter into which they have been resolved, that when struck by the hammer, the impalpable dust set loose sensibly affects the organs of taste and appeals very strongly to those of smell. It is through this saturated rock that the mineral springs take their · course." And again · " The thorough identity of the powerful effluvium that fills the Pump Room with that of the muddy sea-bottom, laid bare in summer weather by the tide, is to the dweller on the seacoast very striking. It *is* identity, not mere resemblance. Here, in smell at least, that ancient mud, swam over by the Diplopterus and Diplacanthus, and in which the Coccosteus and Pterichthys burrowed, has undergone no change. The soft ooze has become solid rock, but its odoriferous qualities have remained unaltered." *

This theory of a " violent movement " of the strata is supported by evidences of upheaval along the northern side of the valley. Even the great fissure of the Raven Rock is regarded by some as a vast rent, with down-throw to the north, whilst others maintain it was cut out by water. But there are undoubted geologic " faults " observing the same direction, in the con-glomerate near Dingwall, and most remarkable of all—the chasm known as the " Black Rock " at Evanton. This occurs in the same formation, and is by most geologists also regarded as a fault.†

---

* *Rambles of a Geologist*, p. 373.

† In all probability this fissure has been caused by "a fault in

The bituminous substance already mentioned as occurring in the Strathpeffer shales was long since observed, and described as a thin vein of coal-like material at the back of Castle Leod. The vein was, indeed, worked more than once, and the masses of black, highly-combustible mineral—now known as *albertite*—used for fuel. Much geological interest has been excited by the discovery that the vein of albertite occupies a narrow fissure in the primary rock. The subject has been latterly treated by Mr. Morrison of Dingwall.* He places albertite between coal and asphalte ; and, in spite of its occasional occurrence, as at Castle Leod, in the gneissose rock, refers it to the Old Red Sandstone. According to this authority, its presence in both formations is due to a fusion of the albertite by heat, developed during the contortion and compression of the rocks. The bituminous fluid would thus be driven, under pressure, into cracks and fissures in the *under*-lying, as well as the *over*-lying, strata. On the banks of the Skiach burn on Ben

the conglomerate, similar to many of those faults which, in the coal measures of the southern districts, we find occupied by the trap. But, in this northern district, where traps are unknown, it must have been filled up by the boulder clay or some still more ancient accumulation of débris. And, when the land had risen, and the streams, swollen into rivers, flowed along the hollows which they now occupy, the loose rubbish would in the lapse of ages gradually wash downwards to the sea, as the stones thrown from the fields above were washed downwards in a later time ; and thus the deep fissure would ultimately be cleared out."—HUGH MILLER, *op. cit.*

* *Trans. Edinb. Geol. Soc.*, 1884.

Wyvis albertite may be picked up as small lustrous jetty fragments. In the Spa shales it takes the form of a thin glossy black scale, or layer, adherent to the rock. It is regarded, in each case, as " formed by a process of dry distillation from the bituminous fish-bearing flags of the Old Red."

Another object of interest in the Spa shales is the nugget or nut of iron pyrites (sulphide of iron). These nuggets, bright and metallic-looking in appearance, are frequently met with in the neighbourhood of the Wells, and testify to the strong sulphureous impregnation of the rocks.

The soil in the lower part of the Strath is alluvial and of great fertility. It is in this, geologically the *most recent* deposit, that one finds the flint arrow-heads and other relics of pre-historic men.

The marks of *Glacial Action* are plentiful around Strathpeffer. Very pronounced scoring and polishing of the rocks may be seen, for example, on the roadside by Rogie Falls, and also a little short of Garve. Glacier drifts abound, some good specimens occurring between Loch Achilty and Little Scatwell. Wandered Boulders, dropped from huge ice-floes when the country was more or less submerged, are met with in all situations, testifying by their alien structure to the remoteness of their origin. In some places the ancient presence of a water line is indicated by *Raised Terraces*, or *Beaches*. These consist of level banks of water-rolled pebbles and sand. Some fine examples occur between Rogie and Contin, beside the Blackwater; and they are seen in great perfection near Auchnasheen and on Loch Curron.

The lover of minerals may enjoy "a happy hunting ground" in the railway cuttings near the Raven Rock and in the adjacent quarry. He will here find fine specimens of *mica* (muscovite) and beautiful *garnets* and *tourmaline*. Near Garve the rare *epidope* occurs on the left-hand side of the road, and *zoisite* in a vein of quartz on the hillside not far from the station.

(2) BOTANY.

The most important influence affecting the flora of a district is undoubtedly *Climate*. In the case of Strathpeffer the presence of mountains and valleys, and the proximity of sea, impart to it a semi-alpine and semi-maritime character; whilst the low rainfall (for a mountainous district) does not admit of that green wealth of foliage and ferns and mosses, characteristic of some of the Western Islands and of the English Lakes. For moist habitats one must here go to the most sheltered woods, and to the rocky dells and corries of the hills, but in these a variety of ferns and many exquisite mosses abound. The sides of Ben Wyvis and Sgurr Maire exhibit, like a miniature Switzerland, the peculiar features of the flora of higher levels—tufted and stunted plants with brightly coloured flowers and berries. Next to climate as a factor in determining the flora is *Geology*. A variety in the geological formation is favourable to variety in the vegetable life which it supports; and the

10

botanical richness of Strathpeffer, as of some parts of Kent, may be partly attributable to this circumstance.

Among the more favoured haunts around the Spa may be mentioned the woods of Brahan and of the Cat's Back, Tor Achilty (where the conglomerate formation ceases towards the west), Rogie, Sgurr Mairc and Ben Wyvis.

The following list comprises some of the less common species met with in the neighbourhood:—*Trollius Europœus,* the Globe flower (Garve); *Thalictrum alpinum* (Sgurr Mairc); *Nymphœa alba* (Achilty); *Corydalis claviculata* (Brahan Woods); *Fumaria officinalis; Eryophila verna* (Nutwood); *Sagina subulata; Hypericum pulchrum; Genista anglica; Rubus chamœmorus,* the Cloudberry (Sgurr Mairc and Ben Wyvis); *Prunus padus,* the Bird-cherry and *avium* the Gean; *Parnassia palustris,* the Grass of Parnassus; *Saxifraga aizoides, granulata* (Kilmorack) and *oppositifolia* (Ben Wyvis); *Epilobium parviflorum* and *palustre; Drosera rotundifolia* and *anglica,* the Sundews (Craig Ulladaile); *Circœa alpina* (Sgurr Mairc); *Linnœa Borealis* (Brahan); *Gnaphalium norvegicum; Tanacetum vulgare* (Fodderty); *Hieracium pilosella, nigrescens* (Brahan) and *Lawsoni* (Knock Farril); *Pyrola media* and *uniflora* (Coul);

---

* The mark * indicates species which the Author has not as yet himself observed. He will, therefore, be grateful for any further observations that visitors may incline to make in the district, which is full of interest to the lover of plants, and at present only partially explored.

Campanula latifolia; Vaccinium myrtillus and *vitis idæa,* the Whortle- and Cow- berry; *Arctostaphylos uva ursi,* the Bearberry, and ** alpina* (Ben Wyvis and Sgurr Mairc); ** Loiseleuria procumbens* (Ben Wyvis); *Lobelia Dortmanna* (Loch Achilty); *Gentiana campestris; Meny-anthes trifoliata,* the Buck-bean; *Myosotis lingulata; Anchusa sempervirens,* Alkanet; *Mimulus luteus* (Contin); *Veronica officinalis* and *arvensis* (Brahan) and *hederifolia; Pinguicula vulgaris,* Butterwort and *lusitanica,* the pale Butterwort (Rogie); *Trientalis Europæa,* the Chickweed Winter-green (Coul); *Juniperus communis; Myrica Gale,* Bog Myrtle; ** Betula nana* (Ben Wyvis and Sgurr Mairc).

Among Orchids: *Gymnadenia conopsea,* the Fragrant Orchis; *Habenaria bifolia* and *viridis,* the Butterfly and Frog Orchis; *Listera ovata* and *cordata,* the Twayblades (all at Coul); ** Corallorhiza innata,* Coral Root; and ** Malaxis paludosa,* the Bog Orchis. *Iris pseudacorus,* the Yellow Iris; *Potamogeton natans,* Pondweed; *Narthecium ossifragum; Scilla nutans* (Craig Ulladaile); ** Alopecurus alpinus,* the Foxtail Grass (Ben Wyvis); *Lycopodium alpinum,* the Alpine Club Moss (Craig Ulladaile) and ** inundatum* (Coul). Among Ferns: *Pteris aquilina,* the Brake; *Lomaria spicant,* the Hard Fern; *Asplenium tricomanes,* Maidenhair Spleenwort; *Filix fæmina,* the Lady Fern; *Adiantum nigrum* and *viride* (the last two at Slumbay); *Nephrodium Filix mas,*

---

* *Vide* note, p. 146.

the Male Fern ; *Spinulosum, Dilatatum* and *Oreopteris,* the Sweet Mountain Fern (all abundant in the wood at the Cat's Back) ; *Polypodium vulgare, Phegopteris,* the Beech, and *Dryopteris,* the Oak Fern (these are found at Rogie, under shady rocks on Craig Ulladaile, and in the Coul woods) ; *Aspidium lonchitis* (Coul).

CHAPTER XIII.

THE district of Strathpeffer is rich in ancient remains. What is called a *stone circle* may be seen on the roadside near Loch Achilty. There is a central mound, probably once the scene of some religious rites, surrounded by a deep ditch, evidently at one time filled with water from the Loch. In the Moy Wood, south west of the Cat's Back Hill, may be found a rounded elevation, or *barrow*, which no doubt marks some ancient burial-place. On the summit is a group of *standing stones*, without marks, rudely arranged in two adjacent circles. There is a similar mound, also crowned by large standing stones, near the boundary of the Cromarty and Tulloch estates, on the heights of Brae, between Strathpeffer and Dingwall. Not very many years since a suicide was buried near this spot, and the passer-by does not neglect to cast a stone upon his grave according to the traditional custom of the country. The curious may discover another suicide's grave by Kinellan, near the pathway to the View Rock. In the folk-lore of the "heights," the barrow on Brae is connected with weird scenes.

It is among the stones on its summit that the De'il
gathers his family on great occasions to drink whisky ;
whilst on a neighbouring hillock it is averred that the
fairies dance at Hallowe'en.

On the Millbuie in the Black Isle, within easy driving
distance of Strathpeffer, there are numerous *cairns* and
tumuli, particularly a group with a fine stone circle above
Kilcoy Castle, and others near the Free Church of
Ferintosh.

There are also, on the mainland : another circle a
little to the east of Alness ; a single stone on the sea-
shore between Alness and Invergordon ; a beautifully
sculptured stone in the grounds of Invergordon Castle ;
and others in the churchyard at Fearn and at Nigg.
One of the finest circles in Scotland is to be seen at
Callernish in the island of Lewis.

The "*Eaglestone*" or "Turning Stone" (*Clach-an-
tionndadh*), is represented on the title-page. It is said
to mark the spot where "the battle turned" in an
old clan feud. The tradition is that the Lady of Seaforth
(Mackenzie) dwelt in a wicker house on the island in
Loch Kinellan. The Munroes of Fowlis carried off
house and lady in her lord's absence, but were overtaken
and defeated by the Mackenzies where the Eaglestone
now stands. The late Rev. Dr. Longmuir regarded
this sculptured stone as belonging to a much more
ancient period. The interpretation is somewhat poetical
—the eagle denotes power and the delineation above
it indicates heaven.

At Drummond, near Fowlis, a barrow has been recently explored, and remains of great interest discovered. 'In two places were found rude "*cists*" or vaults, between three and four feet in length and about two feet in depth, built and covered with rough stone slabs. In each cist there was a skeleton, one of them a woman's,* and in addition an urn, decorated with herring-bone ornamentation, together with the remains of a bronze pin. Similar prehistoric graves were opened at Dalmore, near Alness, in 1878. They contained

---

* The following verses. suggested by this discovery, are here, by the author's permission, appended. Although the reader will perhaps hardly venture so far on the thin ice of Imagination. yet the honoured position of the skeleton does seem to afford some ground for the legend.

With twenty buried centuries,
　Or twice as much, 'neath circled mound
The skeleton in darkness lies,
　Peaceful in the inviolate ground.

A woman's bones, of slender grace,
　Perhaps a Queen's, for whom they made
In tears this hilly burial-place,
　And in rude vault her body laid.

Her head upon her hand at rest,
　Her face toward the eastern sea
Waiting the Dawn—the new, old quest
　Of night-o'erta'en humanity!

Slow the sped Spirit drinks the Light—
　As once her golden flowing hair
The Sun,—and in that radiance bright
　Perchance She is, as then, most fair!

besides skeletons, rude cinerary urns, flint implements, bronze pins, and, what is particularly interesting, one of them a bead necklace of albertite (*vide'* Geology). Barrows, or tumuli, of the same appearance are to be seen on the side of Ben Wyvis and in the Bealloch Mohr, or great pass. It is important to remember that not all structures of this kind are equally ancient. This arises from the habit already alluded to of casting a stone upon a well-known grave.

The ancient burial-place of the house of Cromarty is at Dingwall, and is unmistakable with its leaning monument. At *Press Maree* on the Coul estate there are some curious "*cupped stones.*" The same sort of markings may be seen at the gate of Kinnahaird Farm and elsewhere. Perhaps the most remarkable cupped stone in the district is the face or slab of rock at the side of the path on the ascent of Ben Wyvis about a mile above the railway. This stone exhibits nearly a hundred

---

Yet still our Thought, which may not bide
  In Time's enclosures, joys to rove
Backward as now—The country side,
  Clothed with primæval oaken grove,

Thee homage and thy table food,
  Fair Queen, with plenty, doth endow,
And in the midst a life of Good
  And simple Faith and Honour Thou!

Could but thy relics speak of thee!
  We only know thy race was run,
And that beside the eternal sea
  They laid thee t'ward the rising sun.

cup-markings, some of them double. It is almost certain that it was connected with some superstitious rites, some lingering traces of which appear to survive, for in our own time what seem to be offerings of food have been found laid in these cups. There are, beside Fodderty Church, two standing stones—one of them deeply cupped. Tradition says that these stones were hurled by the Fions from the summit of Knock Farril. They were aimed at the opposing hills, but unfortunately slipped in the hand. The " cup-mark " remains to testify to the size and strength of a Fion's thumb.

There is another class of remains of an exceedingly interesting kind, which carry the mind to an extremely early date, to an age preceding the use of metals. This is the class of " *stone implements* " which are frequently found in the district of Strathpeffer. Among them may be named flint arrow heads, popularly known as " Fairy Darts," stone spear heads and axe-heads, hammers and knives, sinking stones, whorls, slinging balls, etc. It is remarkable that in all countries remains of this kind are connected with the supernatural. Many such implements have thus been prized as possessing miraculous curative powers, even by cultivated persons. This may perhaps arise from their intensely human associations. But here also, all are not equally ancient. In some outlying districts and in the islands it is said that stone implements are still in use, and therefore manufactured from time to time. The most remarkable of these is the

" *Quern,*" or hand-mill, for grinding corn. It consists essentially of two circular stones made to rotate one upon the other. The same form of hand-mill was, according to Julius Cæsar, in use among the Britons in his time, and there is little doubt that it was familiar to the Egyptians in the time of Moses. The use of the quern is a relic of a custom not only most ancient and primitive but widespread.

Yet other, though very different, remains, that carry the interesting halo of antiquity may here be named. These are the stumps of ancient oaks. In a few places, as above Loch Luichart, are still to be seen these relics of that " primæval forest " to which reference has been made.

CHAPTER XIV.

ACCOMMODATION.—This has been very much improved of recent years. The *Ben Wyvis Hotel*, built in 1879, is the largest of the hotels. It is situated above the railway station, and commands a fine view of the mountain from which it is named. The *Spa Hotel*, which has been lately very much enlarged, is on the high ground at the head of the valley, above the Spa. Besides these, there is the comfortable *Private Hotel* (MacGregor's); the old established *Strathpeffer Hotel*, now considerably extended; and the new *Royal Hotel*. Private lodgings, according to taste, are obtainable at the numerous villas. The higher situations are to be more particularly commended for invalids. There is a want of smaller villas, which could be let entire to family parties, who frequently wish to bring their own servants and stay perhaps for several months. What is called the "*Season*" at Strathpeffer is an arbitrary term dictated mainly by convenience and fashion. The waters are not then stronger, or benefit to health more certain, than at other times. Many invalids, indeed, do

well to *avoid* the height of the season, and those in
particular who may wish to consider economy will be in
every way better served either in the early months
(April to June) or in the later Autumn.

Railway Access.—The Spa is eight hours from Edinburgh and seventeen from London.   When the Forth
Bridge is open a considerable shortening of the journey
will be effected.   A favourite train from London is the
8 p.m. from King's Cross, passing through Edinburgh in
the early morning, and reaching Strathpeffer in time for
lunch.   Passengers change at Dingwall.

Drainage and Water Supply.—To meet the rapidly
growing needs of the place, the drainage has been
entirely relaid on a large scale.   The works, which are
ample and on an approved pattern, have been recently
completed.   A new water supply has been brought
from Ben Wyvis.

Amusements.—A good **Band** plays during the season.
Amateur Concerts and other entertainments are given
from time to time in the Pavilion.   Those inclined to
outdoor recreations will find *Bowling Greens* and *Tennis
Lawns* in the neighbourhood of the Spa.   Quite lately
a fine **Golf Course** has been opened behind the Kinettas
Hill.   This course is not without some " hazards " and
gives a most enjoyable game.   The Strathpeffer *Highland Games* are held in the park of Castle Leod in

August, and have hitherto attracted a large concourse of spectators.

Angling.—Angling rights are somewhat limited within walking distance of the Spa, excepting for visitors at the Ben Wyvis or Spa Hotels. Those residing at the former have the privilege of access to the lower reaches of the Blackwater, from Achilty Bridge to the junction with the Conan at Moy. Trout and grilse and an occasional salmon may be got. Anglers from the Spa Hotel have the same opportunities on the Blackwater above Rogie Falls, and the further right of trout-fishing on Loch Garve, which is, however, almost beyond walking distance. All visitors may fish in the Peffery, in which there are small burn trout, four or five to the pound; and also in the Rogie burn, which branches off from the Peffery beyond the Raven's Rock and flows down to the Blackwater near Rogie farm. There is fair trouting also on the Skiach burn, which flows on a north-easterly direction close behind the heights of Auchterneed. Within driving distance visitors have been sometimes permitted to fish in Loch Achilty and Loch Tarvie, and also in the river Conan above the falls, and in the lower end of Loch Luichart whence the Conan flows. Along the Skye Railway visitors at Strathpeffer may obtain permission to fish the Garve river (from Garve Station); the rivers Grudie and Bran and perhaps Loch Culen (from Loch Luichart Station); Loch Achanault, in which there is very good trout-fishing (from Achanault Station) and finally, from Auchnasheen Station, the little river Sheen.

Library, etc.—There is a circulating library, with some of the most recent works, under the care of Miss MacLean at the Fancy Repository. Daily papers may be seen at the Pavilion. Water drinkers have the free use of the hall.

Churches.—Two new Churches (of the Established and Free Presbyterian bodies respectively) testify not only to the energy of religious organization, but to the increased importance of the field. The Church of England services are at present conducted weekly in the Pavilion, until a sufficient fund has been collected for providing a more suitable edifice.

Postal Arrangements.—Mails are despatched : 7·35 a.m., 12·45 p.m., 4·30 p.m. Letters are delivered : 11·0 a.m., 1·30 p.m., and (after June 1st) 4·45 p.m. The Telegraph Office is open throughout the day.

INDEX.

FINIS.

THE LEAMINGTON WATERS CHEMICALLY,

THERAPEUTICALLY, AND CLINICALLY CONSI-
DERED; with Observations on the Climate of Leamington.
By FRANCIS WILLIAM SMITH, M.D. Second Edition.
Crown 8vo, with Illustrations, 1s. *nett.*

"We commend the book to the attention both of doctors and patients."
—*The Times.*

"Dr. Smith's book will be found useful by all who meditate a visit to
Leamington, and by those who are hesitating regarding the choice of a
suitable resort."—*Health.*

"We trust that Dr. Smith's little treatise, written in a lively and popular
style, will contribute to the very desirable end of bringing patients back
to Leamington—a very useful medical guide."—*London Medical Record.*

ROYAT (LES BAINS) IN AUVERGNE, ITS

MINERAL WATERS AND CLIMATE. By G. H.
BRANDT, M.D. With Frontispiece and Map. Second Edition.
Crown 8vo, 2s. 6d.

BY THE SAME AUTHOR.

HAMMAM R'IRHA, ALGIERS. A Winter Health

Resort and Mineral Water Cure Combined. With Frontispiece
and Map. Crown 8vo, 2s. 6d.

ILLUSTRATED LECTURES ON AMBULANCE

WORK. By R. LAWTON ROBERTS, M.D., M.R.C.S.
Copiously Illustrated. Third Edition. Crown 8vo, 2s. 6d.

"The descriptions are in clear intelligible language, and there is a
laudable absence of those long-sounding words with which we too often
meet in lectures which are intended to be popular."—*Lancet.*

"Among works of this class Dr. Lawton Roberts' deserves a high place.
All his descriptions are clear, he dwells upon the points of importance,
and omits every detail which does not add to the precise instruction he
wishes to convey. Every part of the book is good. The lucid text is made
clearer still by well-chosen and well-drawn woodcuts, and in the 164
pages scarcely a superfluous sentence is to be found."—*Athenæum.*

AMBULANCE LECTURES: Nursing. By Samuel Osborn, F.R.C.S., Assistant-Surgeon, Hospital for Women; Surgeon, Royal Naval Artillery Volunteers. With Illustrations. Fcap. 8vo, 1s. 6d.

COMPANION VOLUME BY THE SAME AUTHOR.

AMBULANCE LECTURES: First Aid. Fcap. 8vo, 1s. 6d.

"Two handy little volumes . . . . give compactly, and in small space, information as useful in the home as in the hospital."—*The Graphic.*

THE HEALTH OF CHILDREN. By Angel Money, M.D., B.S., M.R.C.P., Assistant Physician to the Hospital for Sick Children, and to University College Hospital, etc. Crown 8vo, 6d.

"It is written in simple language, and the information, which is concisely put, is just that which is required by every one who has the care of young children. . . . Every mother should possess a copy of this excellent treatise, and its small price places it within the reach of all."—*Saturday Review.*

DISINFECTANTS AND HOW TO USE THEM. By E. T. Wilson, B.M. Oxon., F.R.C.P. Lond., Physician to the Cheltenham General Hospital and Dispensary. In packets of one dozen, price 1s.

*** These cards will be found particularly suitable for heads of families, clergymen, and nurses : or for distribution among the artizans and tradesmen of our larger towns.

"This little card is one of the most valuable aids in the diffusion of health knowledge that we remember to have seen. Clergymen, and all others interested in the welfare of the people, could not do a wiser thing than distribute them broadcast."—*Health.*

BATH, CONTREXEVILLE, AND THE LIME SULPHATED WATERS. By John Macpherson, M.D., Inspector-General of Hospitals H.M. Bengal Army (Retired). Author of "Cholera in its Home," etc. Crown 8vo, 2s. 6d.

H. K. LEWIS, 136, GOWER STREET, W.C.